Red Reign

by

Jason Blacker

PUBLISHED BY:
Lemon Tree Publishing
Copyright © 2014
Jason Blacker

Visit www.JasonBlacker.com on the web to stay up to date

Editing: Andrea Anesi

ISBN: 9781927623558

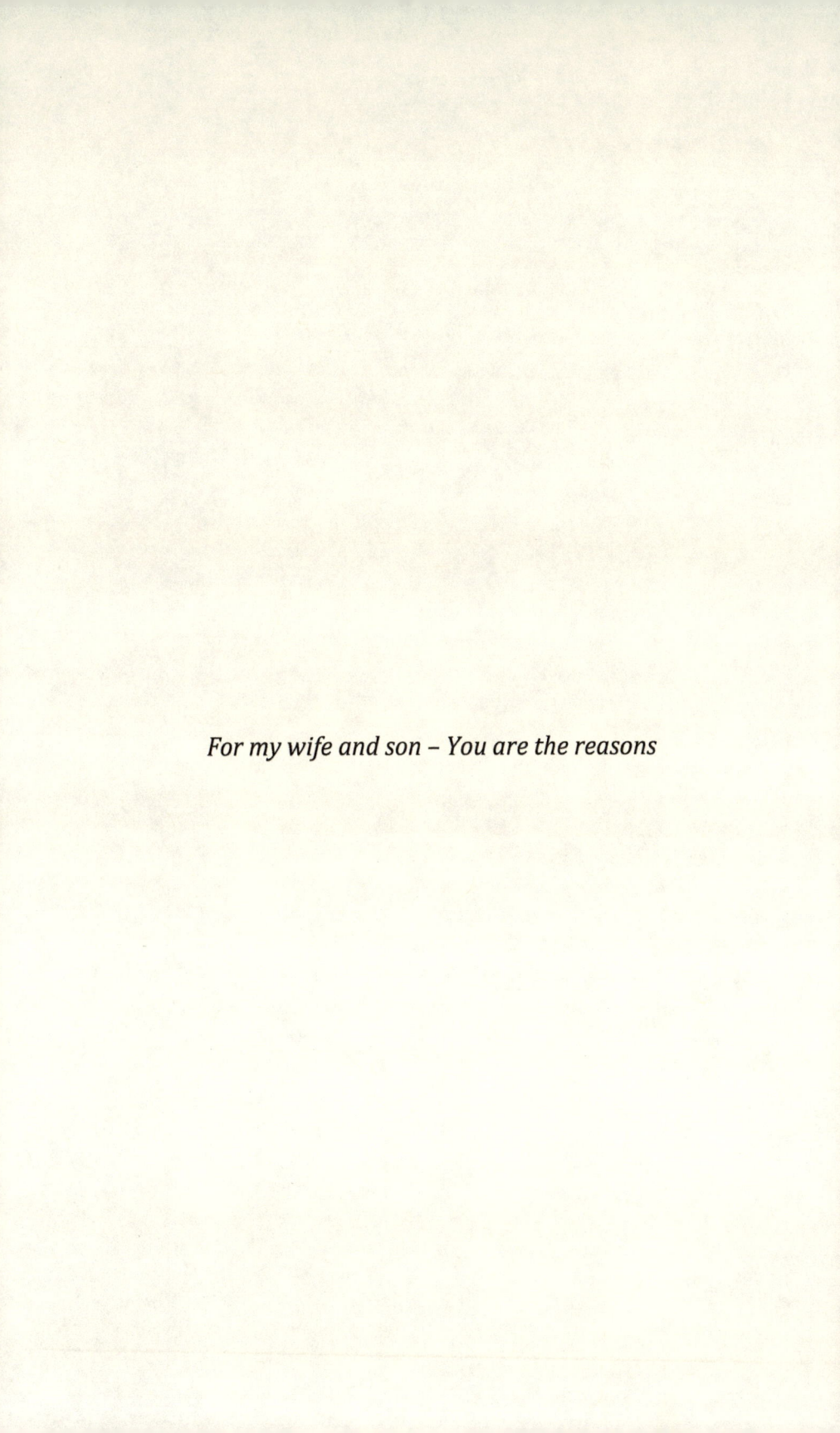

For my wife and son – You are the reasons

Table of Contents

The End

I want to tell a story that's important to me. I hope by the end of me telling it it'll be important to you too. I'm going to tell it from the end and work my way back to the beginning. Maybe that way when you're thinking about starting out on a course you might choose better than they did here. Maybe if I tell it this way you'll hear it better and things just might change. This isn't an easy story for me to tell and you'll figure out why at the end. I don't want to give too much away right from the start. You've got to follow me all the way back to the beginning for this to make sense. And I'll reward you for your time. I'll see to that.

But just so you know where we are let me explain it to you. We're in a holding cell here in a New York Police precinct. There's a guy sitting by himself off to one corner. If you're looking at the cell he's to your right. His legs are straight out in front of him. Looks awkward and uncomfortable. But he doesn't seem to mind. You see he's taken this shirt he was wearing. A nice white oxford. Expensive. You can tell by the quality of the cloth. It's thick but soft. He's not wearing the oxford how you're supposed to. He's wrapped it around his neck tight. And he tied it to one of the bars. Really tight. And his head is swollen and puffy and going plum purple. It's not a pretty site. He's been dead less than five minutes. He did this to himself and he didn't struggle. Well that's a bit of a lie. He struggled involuntarily as the body does when it's dying. But he didn't claw at the shirt. There are no scratches on his neck. You could have a look if you wanted to. But I wouldn't encourage that. Take my word for it. His eyes are bulged out like white squash balls. He liked that game. He liked playing squash. You can tell that too by his trim physique. He's wearing a white tank top as an undershirt. Some circles call it a wife beater. But it's nothing like that. He loved his wife. He loved his family. We'll get to that in a minute. That was part of the problem. Part of the problem as to why he's lying here his head cocked at a crooked angle like a dog does when they're trying to figure something out. This fellow's done figuring now. He'd done too much. Maybe the wrong kind and this is also why he got to be here like this. As a specimen for me to mention. And I don't mean any disrespect when I say it like that. He wouldn't mind. He wants his story told. He doesn't want other folks to go through this.

You're probably wondering what the guy's name is. I should give you that much if I'm going to ask you to come on this journey with me. This backwards tale. Not that knowing his name will make a difference but it might. It might make you feel it more. And if you can feel it more by the time we're done. Then maybe it won't happen again. His name is Regin Sigurd. Regin like the former president Reagan. Sigurd is as it sounds. He's been in this cell by himself for about two hours now. If there had been company he might not have done this. And he certainly wouldn't have succeeded. The guards come by every fifteen minutes. That might change after the public inquiry that will happen. But it's nobody's fault. You can't stop people from killing themselves if they're really intent. And he doesn't want anyone blamed for this. He knows this lies squarely on his own shoulders. There's been enough heartache already. Besides we're at the end of this story. As we track back you'll discover how much there's been. Enough for an eternity on a planet as beautiful as ours. And he was thinking about that before he died. About this beautiful planet of ours. He was thinking about all this pain set amongst all this beauty. Like one red poppy squashed between white pages. That was the actual image in his mind before he took his life. Sad and beautiful at the same time isn't it?

His hands are like two long sausages lying limp from his shoulders. Like someone stuck them on there like putty. His hands are lying palms up fingers pointing the same direction as his legs. They look like ashtrays. Like what people did with gorillas' hands before they knew better. Before we started understanding things better. Our role in the world maybe. But that's another story. Regin's ankles are sticking out of dark blue slacks. His feet forming a V between them. V for victory but there's no real victor in this story. I'm telling you all of this because it all looks curious. Like it might not be real. If you could see it from where I am. Like an outside observer. You lose the emotional attachment to the event. I'm hoping we'll find that together during this journey. We need to. Without empathy how can anything ever change? If it was always survival of the fittest. Or as Gandhi said an eye for an eye would leave the whole world blind. And he got that. Regin did. Just before he died. He understood that. The interconnectedness of everything. The butterfly's wings causing the tsunami. He got that. But that was during his last moments. His last few breaths. Count them. Three. His last three breaths. The butterfly effect I think they call it. How everything matters. Even the smallest occurrences can change the universe forever. That's powerful stuff. He got that then in his last breaths. But he didn't reach further. He couldn't see the result of that equation. That even he was flapping his butterfly wings as he ended his life. Things might have been different for him. For a whole bunch of people. This is what this story is about. This is why I'm hoping that by telling it the wrong way backwards maybe things will end up right next time.

Let's pause to think about things. Think about consequences. Choices. There are always choices. Did this guy make the right choice the best choice in strangling himself? I'll ask you to be the judge of that by the end. But there were other choices. Always are. This is not for me to judge though I have opinions on it. I'll try keeping them to myself but I can't promise that. But I'm the narrator here of a deathly tale. That's my first obligation and the one I'll try do justice to. There are a lot of noises around here. At this police precinct. As I suppose there should be. But it's quiet. It's two thirty in the morning. Thursday morning. Not even a weekend. You can hear other inmates urinating and talking. More like murmuring. You can't really make anything out. Not all the cells are full. Some are empty but most have at least two people in them. You can hear the guards. They're probably really police officers come by every once in a while. But some of this stuff is new to me. And I don't pretend to know it all. But as long as you get the gist I'll be happy. I'm not trying to give an accurate account of the details. It's the broad facts that are more important in this tale. So please forgive me some of these errors in advance. I don't want you worrying about errors of detail. This is a story about people and tragedy. That's the focus here. The people and their stories. Their intertwined and tangled webs. So you can hear the guards come by once in a while. Their boots thwacking on the tiled floors. It's not so much ominous as welcoming really. Knowing that someone is coming by to check on your welfare. Even if they don't give a damn about you you know it's their public duty to do the right thing. And you can count on that. To a large degree anyway. And most of the cells can be seen on a video monitor in the office. But the one our fellow is in just happens not to be working. So that didn't help.

And even if it did they're busy around here and not as vigilant at looking at the monitors as they could be.

So there isn't much time to tell this story so you'll see I'll tend to jump around some. Maybe ramble and come back on track. Telling this story from the present into the past also means it'll be one long tale. It needs that. Honesty dictates I tell it to you directly as I know it. Straight from me to you. No worrying and being diluted by storytelling guidelines and conventions. I trust that'll be okay. I figure I can tell it straight enough that you'll follow along okay. I believe it because I need to. This story needs to reach you at a deeper level. Something else I should tell you about this man. He was married I told you that. Had a nineteen year old daughter. Her name was Frea but pronounced free. We'll get to her and his wife a little later. They were all good people full of potential. Like all of us. But they weren't bent. Weren't mean spirited. Regin's wife's name was Moana. This means wide expanse of water in Maori. Her parents were New Zealanders and loved the name. It suited her too. You'll understand why as we go along. They were married twenty-five years to the day. Not to this day. This is the day he died. They were married twenty-five years to the day his wife and daughter died. Were murdered actually. But this is not a cozy mystery story. I'll tell you who did it soon enough and why. This is about people and their stories. Not a whodunit. Anyway one step at a time. We're still here with our fellow. With Regin. Even standing a couple of feet away from him you can smell it. The booze. He's inebriated. That's why he's here. Well partly why he also crashed while driving home. Hit a young woman in her car when he blew a red light. He didn't see it. The red light or her. He was tested at point two. Almost three times the legal limit. Funny thing is he's not really a drinker. He'd hardly ever drink. Maybe on occasion a beer or wine. At most two but no more. And I don't mean any disrespect when I say it's funny. Because I mean in a tragic way. But you can probably tell.

Her name was Adrasteia. Same age as Frea. Lovely girl. We'll get to know more about her too. This is a tragedy. This whole tale of events just one big tragedy. But I want to leave you with hope. The hope that things can be different. If we see how they unraveled and get back to the beginning to the purity. We can do it better. Trust me. We can do it right. And by the time I tell you all this you'll know why I'm so confident we can do it right. Why I believe in this potential. This human potential if you will. But I'm going to have to omit certain things. I mean I could keep telling this story to the end of eternity if we kept pulling at the thread. This fabric of life this universal blanket that all of us are tied to. If we unravel it long enough you'll see it'll unravel and catch us all along its length. This is the butterfly effect I was talking about earlier. Really it's true. Take Adrasteia for example. We can explore that line and the effect her death had on her parents. Both of them still alive. You're not supposed to bury your own children. So maybe the dad takes to drinking. Gets fired and starts beating on his wife. She takes up with another man her husband finds out and kills them both. I mean this could happen. Not to put the blame on our fellow in the cell. But we've got to understand the repercussions. Try and live a little more honestly and kindly. Give each other a leg up rather than a kick in the teeth. Now I could tell you what happens to Adrasteia's parents. I'm privy to this now from where I am. I can see the whole universe unfolding into the future and then unfolding again and again. This is happening trillions upon trillions upon trillions of times a second. All because we're constantly making choices and unraveling the future and then again in a different way as it all coincides as it all mushes up together like paint smeared on canvas. It's beautiful really. A real sight to behold. The brilliance of it all. The majesty the omniscience of it. It's hard to really describe as I look at it. Just pure brilliance and joy and peace and song and love and beauty and goodness all squashed up and unfolding like a beautiful fragrant flower in your hand. That maybe gives you an inkling of it all. That's why I'm so adamant about understanding our choices. Trying to be better. Because from where I am it's hugely important. It's the very fabric of existence. The very song of the universe. It's life or death really. And not just for us but for the whole spiritual plane.

So as I was saying I could tell you about other people. About Adrasteia's parents her boyfriend and what not. But that'd just make the story longer and it'll be plenty long enough as it is. And I think it'll also dilute the message the flavor of what I'm trying to tell. And I don't want that. I want this story. This tale of lives of beautiful souls to tear open your heart so the bleeding rivers of pain can only be stanched by the gauze of universal kinship and love. I'm sorry to go on like this. But you have no idea how paramount this need is. Not for me. I'm just telling the tale. My life is over and I'm on the other side. But you who are living need fair warning. You need to not repeat the errors of us who have gone before. You can never be too full of kindness nor too empty of meanness. Honestly. That's from the highest order. So Regin sits now. Just a shell. His body waiting to be given back to the earth. And the body should be given back to the earth. It should be wrapped up in muslin and he should be put in the earth and covered up and digested by the earth. The body is from earth and it should be returned there. The soul has already gone home. Back from where it came to journey on in different dimensions in different incarnations to grow to seek love and to connect ever closer to the whole. The body can also be burned with fire and scattered across the earth. That would be appropriate too. And our fellow here would want that. If you could ask him that. Of course you can't but if you could he'd agree with what I'm saying. Only that won't happen to him. He'd made prior arrangements. He had planned for the inevitable. His will dictates that he be laid in a coffin next to his wife and daughter. A nice coffin airtight and with the embalming he'd chosen you could dig him up in a hundred years and there wouldn't be much decomposition. Macabre really if you ask me. But I've told you what I think should happen and he'd agree now only he's made prior arrangements and nothing can be done about that from this side of the window. This side of the pane.

They're bringing in more people to the precinct every minute it seems. People making poor decisions. I'm rushing to tell my tale and they're bringing in people quicker than I can try and convince you to change. But I have my hopes too. I've seen the power of knowledge and of love and of the capacity to change. So I'm not worried about it. I just have an urgency to my call. I'll need to be going soon too. But I think they'll give me time to finish this up. It's important. Everyone if you can call them that though they frown on the individualizing of the whole recognizes the importance of more of us taking a different course. So the police bring in more people and we try to steer more away. We're winning by the way. If you were wondering. We're winning the battle and the war. Just seems slow sometimes when you're watching eternity unfold. But the quicker we do it the quicker all of us get to more important work.

So while we wait for one of the guards to realize our poor man is dead I'll tell you a little more about him. He had a good job in an oil company in town here. He was a VP of international development. But that was before. They paid him well too. Lots of money and he liked his job too but some of the things gave him pause. Didn't sit well with him. But the bonuses helped assuage any guilt he might have. And he loved the look on his wife's face when he'd buy her nice things. When he could spoil his wife and daughter. His job helped pay for so many fond memories. Disneyland when Frea was nine years old. That was

one of the highlights. Amongst many others. And she's just
finished sophomore year at Yale which he was paying for thanks
to work. But he hadn't worked since Sunday the thirtieth of
January. By that time he was CEO. But we'll get to that. The day
Frea and Moana died. The day he died in a metaphorical sense.
But he could've tried a different route. I don't mean to be
condescending saying that but he could've. He didn't. Not that it's
easy. It's hard I understand that to lose the two most important
people in your life. You need to take time out. Pause and catch
your breath. You need to gather yourself towards yourself as my
mother would say. Ask for help. Call on others for strength and
nurturing. We don't do that much. That's one of our downfalls.
We want to be strong and we're proud and we want to be brave
and rugged on the frontier of life. But that's not how it works.
We're all one. All part of the whole. We need to help each other
out. Heed the call. Please remember that for next time.

But we're talking about our friend Regin. He didn't know how
to. Couldn't call for help and it undid him. Slowly like a serpent
constricting around your chest. He allowed the pain and the
suffering and the anguish to extinguish his pain. Squash it into
nothingness. So that his heart as an icon of compassion and love
was crushed into a lump of coal. Dry and hard and dead. And
after that the spirit leaves. It has to. This human experience of
the spirit is a journey of the heart and of healing and of
emotional vibrancy. That sustains it. That is the purpose of this
journey. So he ends up here. Tied to a cell all by himself. Tied by
himself with a white shirt. A nice white shirt that looks now
more like a flag of surrender. And indeed it is. He's surrendered
to the pain. But the journey has only now begun. The lessons
now harder to learn. This was an easy one. Didn't feel like that
for him. I know it sounds almost trite for me to say that. Who am
I you might be asking. But truly this was an easier lesson of the
lessons to be completed. Grade ten as opposed to grade twelve.

I hear the footfalls now. The boots knocking down the hallway. They're quick now. I think they're running they must have seen the video. Get the medic Jack says one of the officers. Jack takes off to get the medic. Don continues on to the cell and releases Regin from his own bindings. He checks for pulse but doesn't find any. They won't find any. The spirit has left. There's nothing they can do for the body now. Don lays Regin down and starts compressions and breaths. The medic arrives he's got the new AED device. Adelmo that's the medic juices up Regin but nothing happens. Nothing will. They try two more times. They're frantic but they're professional this has happened a couple of times for them over their careers but it never gets easier. Adelmo is praying. Padre nuestro que estas en el cielo santificado sea tu Nombre. It's the Our Father. He's whispering it under his breath. Don and Jack aren't paying attention. Jack leaves again to call an ambulance. They need a doctor to pronounce him dead. Adelmo knows already. He can tell. He's been through this before. Well not quite like this. When he was twelve he came across from Cuba with his family. Mother father two brothers and a sister. They all perished. He almost did but somehow made it and after two days adrift just off the coast of Florida was rescued by a rich American in a yacht. The guy's name was Anzu Buer. Why am I telling you this because the world is a small place and Anzu Buer was the founder of the global oil company named Anzu where Regin was the VP of International Development. Anzu brought Adelmo to American soil and he took him to the nearest Catholic Church where Adelmo was fostered out and gained citizenship.

So to get even a little more spooky. Adelmo's name means noble protector. Anzu doesn't know yet Adelmo was saved and Regin can't be. Small world. You couldn't make up stuff like this. Christ Don is saying every so often. Jack comes back with a stretcher and they load our man on it and take him out to the ambulance. Lights and sirens and a short time later our fellow is at the hospital pronounced dead. Adelmo was with him. Jack and Don had to stay back at the precinct. They've all just become a little more jaded. A little more pissed off and a little more bitter about the muck of humanity. This'll affect them and their choices because unfortunately they're not making the best of it. Not understanding the subtleties I'm trying to get across to you. But this story isn't about them it's about our fellow Regin. So I'll try and stay the course. He's gone now. In spirit and in body of course. So we'll move back in time a little bit.

Just to help you we're at two fifty-five in the morning as Regin is getting pronounced. But he actually died at about two thirty or if you want the accurate time it was two twenty-five and fifty-five seconds Eastern Standard Time. It's Thursday ninth of March. This is our starting point. From here we move back.

We're going back to about twelve oh five same evening. Just about fifty-five minutes before another death. The death of Adrasteia. I know there are a lot of deaths in this story. Because it is a story of many deaths. Humans live and they die. This is inevitable. This is how it should be. Please don't be upset about the fact that people are dying in this story. There is nothing wrong with dying it's part of the circle. It's a necessary completion to this journey. The start of a new beginning. So don't mourn the deaths but rather let us mourn the choices that have led to these deaths. It is not the dying but the living up to that dying that is lacking. And this is good news for us who are alive. I shouldn't really say us. I should say you in a plural sense. I'm not really living anymore. Not like you are anyway. So let's seize this opportunity to explore the deficits in these lives in a compassionate way so that we can learn and do better. It's easier this way. Truly it is. You don't want to have to do remedial. It sucks. It sucked when you were in grade six and it sucks even worse if you die prematurely. The lessons then become harder.

So we're tracking back to find our man. He's getting himself plastered. And this is so unlike him. At the beginning of the year and before he would occasionally have a social drink. And not every time either. Now you wouldn't recognize him. He's been drinking since three pm. It's just gone midnight and he's so wasted he's got double vision. Thing is the body gets used to this high consumption quite easily. So that even just a month ago drinking the amount he's had tonight he'd be vomiting already. Not now. He's swaying as he walks to the bathroom. He still dresses up nicely in a business suit as if he's just left work early.

If we track back to just after four we'd see what looks like a dapper man in his early fifties stroll casually into The Carlyle and into Bemelmans' Bar. He's a little taller than average Joe. The police mug shot that was taken later this evening put him at five eleven. But he was slouching. We could give him an even six. He's trim as you know from all the squash he used to play up until about three months ago when the "incident" happened. It's funny how it became referred to as that. He couldn't call it anything else with his psychiatrist. Couldn't actually speak about it outside of those sessions. And as you can imagine this caused his general withdrawal from life and friends. More about that later. But in a way calling death by other names is just avoidance. And by avoiding things you give them greater power. They become bigger monsters. Skeletons that creak and rattle in closets too small for discretion. That's something I need to share. Confront the dark nights of your life and shed light into them to clear out the cobwebs and bogeymen.

So he's still trim Regin is because he's mostly on a liquid diet now. A diet of liquor. You'd see him walk in and admire the dark blue suit. The crisp white shirt. The red tie. Color of fresh blood. And if you looked closely you'd see the black stripes across the tie. His unconscious nod to the black armband. He's wearing a nice cologne. It's fresh and spicy you can choose your favorite.

His hair looks wet and it's jet black with touches of gray that men thought was distinguished and ladies just found downright sexy. He's a good looking man. Square jaw deep blue eyes and a wide and vibrant smile. But you won't see that tonight. As he walks by you to take his usual seat up at the edge of the bar you'd catch a whiff of alcohol after the first blush of cologne. He's already well oiled and about to get smashed. He doesn't know any better how to heal the pain. Or rather to numb the pain. Little does he know that this anesthetizing of it with alcohol only feeds it and makes it more unruly.

Some other businessmen are here for a late business meeting. They admire this well kept gent. His seemingly well put together ensemble. His easy stride. Easy only because he's had three vodkas already. Women out together for a drink look and admire him too. Then they turn and whisper quietly to each other about how rich and handsome he must be. It would appear too that he glances around and takes in the scene. But rest assured he doesn't see you. He's looking into the past really. Looking for his wife and daughter.

People being so caught up in themselves and envious and trying to keep up and do better than the other fella only think well of Regin. See him as a man in his prime. His earning prime his career prime. They see a man of wealth and stature and good looks. The women too. But that's because they don't take a moment to look past their envies and jealousies. They don't take a moment to ignore their own small petty egos. If they were in touch with their true selves. Their spiritual connection to the whole they would see that this shell. This very thin veneer that is our fellow is almost transparent it is so thin. So obviously frail. Just a moment to look into his eyes would have you drowning in wells of sorrow so deep and torrid.

So our man can sit at the end of the bar like this for hours with hardly a soul well that's a lie the souls notice but with hardly another person noticing that he is in need. In deep need of compassionate understanding and connection. Instead they pay him no further attention other than as a yardstick of their own material wealth. And our man drinks himself into oblivion. And he's about to end his own and another's life. All for the wanting of a little perseverance. A little understanding. And a little empathy.

So you might be wondering if there is any reason why he keeps coming here to Bemelmans' Bar in The Carlyle. And there are several. It was the bar he wanted to bring Frea to when she turned twenty-one in less than two years time. More importantly Bemelmans' was named after the writer of the Madeline children's books. Great books. If you've never read them you should. The art and the storytelling are excellent. But for our fellow Madeline was Frea's favorite book as a child. She collected the whole series. The original series that Ludwig Bemelmans wrote himself. All six of them.

And if you look at him now. Regin as he sits at the bar he looks at the pictures from the stories painted on the wall here. He brings a tumbler of whiskey to his lips. In an old house in Paris that was covered in vines he says lived twelve little girls in two straight lines he says. You can't really hear him. You'd have to have your ear right up to his mouth. But you can see his lips move. And this is what he says. They left the house at half past nine. The smallest one was Frea he says breaking the rhyme. His eyes are glassy. They're red from the alcohol but now from the pain. A rim of tears swells on his lower lids. He picks up the cocktail napkin and dabs at them. Most times people don't notice. And I say most times because this happens like clockwork every day. And everyday he almost cries but can't. He just can't let himself. Probably because the pain is all he has left of them now. To work through it would mean releasing them. In his mind this is how he thinks. At a deeply subconscious level. So in some perverse way this pain is his attachment to the ones he loved.

You okay fella the bartender asks. Our man looks at his shirt and his name tag says Armen. Yeah Armen I'm fine. Got something in my eye. I'll have another whiskey. Armen looks at him for a while. Giving him a chance to talk. Nothing happens so he goes and gets him his drink. This has happened before but Regin's never taken the time to look at his name tag.

The whiskey arrives. He doesn't notice. He's looking at the pictures of Madeline on the wall. He's seeing his daughter in bed all curled up with her bear. It was a gift he gave her on her birth. She's now seven and the bear is an old panda bear but most of its fur is gone. But she loves it. She's cuddled up with it. The bear's name is Madeline. Frea's eyes are heavy the lids are fluttering. She sucks her thumb and stops. Then starts again. She's falling asleep. That's all there is there isn't anymore he says. He kisses her on the forehead. She murmurs something and he leaves her room turning at the door just to have one last look. Now he sips his whiskey. He wants that one last look again. But it will never be. And he doesn't know how to deal with that. The tears well up again but he stanches them with the napkin. They will not role down his face. He has cried about the loss before. But only privately. Nobody has seen him shed these acid hot tears. Nobody except his psychiatrist. And he wasn't proud of that. He should be stronger. So he thinks. He should be stronger. But it's his attempt at strength that is killing him.

Not that our man notices but the bartender looks over every so often. He can tell something is wrong. But you can't swim in the river of denial without help. And he's dipped his toe in there. But it's frigid. You've seen that. So he leaves Regin alone. He polishes glassware. It's not that busy here tonight. Perhaps it will be later. But not right now. There are only three people at his bar. Regin a younger woman and an old man. The old man is in his sixties but he looks late seventies or eighties. He's a practiced alcoholic. The nose gives it away. A red bulbous thing that looks like it was stuck on. And his thinness. He's been living on the liquid diet most of his life. His name's Chuck. Chuck Stayk and you can imagine how much fun that was for him growing up. His birth certificate said Chuck. Not Charles. He's had a tough life and I won't bore you with the details. But we've got to sprinkle some color in this story. Life's not easy for most people. And most people don't handle it that well. This story aims to help you overcome that. Do a little better if you just stretch a little. So Chuck doesn't have any friends. I say that honestly. That's not exaggeration or hyperbole. There is not a man or woman that he can call friend. He was married once for a year. Happiest year of his life until his wife left him for a woman. That was the straw on the camel's back that was Chuck's life. Enough said about Chuck. He's also committing suicide. Only it will take him another two and a bit years. And hundreds of bottles of vodka.

So Chuck's at the other end of the bar. This young woman. Twenty-four and made up thickly is sitting two stools away from our fellow. Her name is Zonah. She's been here before and seen our man. She likes him and thinks he's loaded. He is but only on liquor. He used to earn a good wage but he's been spending it loosely on liquor mostly and giving it away to shysters. He's not as rich as she hopes. She's come up from Alabama. A white trash kind of girl. And I don't say that unkindly. But she thought she was going to be a pop sensation and hasn't found work. She's this close to living on the streets and prostituting herself out. So instead she's been trolling these upscale bars looking for a sugar daddy. You can't blame her. Her life has been hell. We'll find out more about that soon enough. So a week ago she came in and spent most of the time watching Regin. Other men took interest in her and bought her drinks. This is how it goes. But she only left when he did. He hasn't noticed her yet. She watched him get into his black BMW and then she knew he was the one she wanted. Besides all the other men in here are slobs and letches. They're old and bald and fat. Our man is sexy and handsome. She can see herself with him. So she came back and then she came back again tonight. Tonight is the night she will make her move. She's drinking to shore up her courage. Trying to find that ideal time. She's so wrapped up in this fantasy she's created with our fellow that she can't see his real needs. His real pain. Mind you he's not interested in her story either. He hasn't even noticed her yet. But he will. He will use her as he does this booze. To numb the pain. But I'm getting ahead of myself.

The rest of Bemelmans' isn't too busy either. We've got a few tables of business men winding down from their hard days at the office. Captains of industry. Nice name that. Sounds so heroic. So noble. But there isn't anything noble about most of these men here tonight. Most of them. There are the exceptions of course. Those that prove the rule isn't that what they say. Here's one example. Gier Vautour. That's the guy's name. He can't help it. He's Dutch but came here when he was a baby. He's one of these captains. He's ruining the company he's running. A big named automobile manufacturer. American that shall remain nameless to protect the guilty. Well he's just given himself a huge bonus. Six million dollars he made in bonus last year. And what did he do for that. Well he put nineteen thousand people out of work. He's decimating a community by closing down a plant that was the biggest employer in their town. He's also managed to drive the price of the stock down by over seventy percent. And the cherry on the cake was managing to take a three billion dollar loss. All this in one year. Plus he had the union on its knees when he got concessions to pay new hires fifteen bucks an hour. And that's if they're lucky enough to get a job. Little does he know that he'll be unemployed in less than three months. The board's had enough. But I'm not sorry for him. He'll get a nine million dollar cushion to soften the fall on his lazy ass. He's fat he treats his wife like crap and he kicks the dog. But here he is with his cronies having a good chuckle and crude jokes made about women blacks and Hispanics. Yeah you could say he's a real humanitarian.

Sorry about that. I'm getting myself sidetracked here. It's hard not to when you've got all this knowledge at your finger tips. But it helps me show you how sometimes life seems unfair. But it's not really. If you go back far enough we're all unfolding and growing as we should. But we can make it better. Hasten the growth towards the light instead of remaining mushrooms in the dark.

Armen comes over and gives our man a martini. It's an extra dry vodka martini he says. Should help alleviate any hangover. It's on the house he says. He looks at Regin. He's reaching out smiling. Our man looks up at him. Tries a smile but it won't come. So he says thank you. Armen notices the wedding band on our fellow's finger. Platinum. He still wears it. Attachments you see. He can't let go of anything. I see you're married he says. My fiancé and I are hoping to get married next year he says. Armen is trying. Thinks this guy just needs to talk. That would be a start. He's the only one around here who's trying. God bless him for that. And he will trust me. But the poor lad's put his foot in his mouth without meaning too. I don't want to talk Armen if you don't mind says our man. He's trying not to be stern. But the only feelings he's got nowadays are hatred and anger and sadness against the whole world. Armen tries a smile. A brave attempt but there's no hiding the fact he's hurt. He's been chided. But that's honest. And he'll have a better time at living life if he can continue to live honestly. Especially if he can remain emotionally honest. And he will. I don't want you thinking that everybody here fails. Armen doesn't. Life's not easy. It's not meant to be. That's not why we're here. But the lessons can be learned and the pain overcome with a bit of honesty. Emotional honesty. Sadly the people at the center of this story haven't managed that part of life very well. That's why I've got a story to tell you. But rest assured there is the possibility of success. If you like I'll even let you know that the dice are loaded in your favor. Truly. There are cheat sheets everywhere. All of us are beacons warning flares and guides along the way. For each other. We carry the answers within. Just take a moment. Be still and reflect and you'll find it there. Just like I say. I'll be giving you these tips as we go along. But enough of that for now.

Armen will be all right. He's been called to be a bartender. He will help many people. Even though tonight he is impotent in saving our fellow tomorrow he will say some kind words to a stranger. To someone who has never been in here before. He will have to be tough with him and cut him off. Send him home in a cab. But that stranger who will come in to drink before he goes home to blow his brains out won't do that. Because of what Armen said. And not specifically what he said but that he showed interest in this wayfaring stranger. This man blown in from the harsh streets of life. That's all it takes. You can do as much too. Wherever you are you can help from there. Any interaction with anyone can be the starting point of bringing peace. Do not be misled into believing that you are not rich enough or powerful enough or well known enough to do any good. I promise you. Right now with your heart aware there are boundless opportunities to bring peace and justice to this world. Honestly. I've just told you about Armen. And he is not unique.

So Armen will be all right. He will not be well known. He will never amount to much in a materialistic sense. He will never be rich or good looking though he certainly isn't unpleasant to look at. But he has riches far greater than this world can offer. He has a pure heart and emotional honesty. He has love and joy in his spirit. And he will walk this life as a saint. I promise you. And you can too.

Zonah will too. In time. Right now she's learning. But she will get the hang of it. She will come to see the light. Very soon. Within the next few days as she learns of our fellow's death and his story. My prayer for you is that you can like Zonah like Armen learn from others. Overcome life's burdens and troubles and live with a pure and honest heart. An open and joyful spirit. I know you can. Otherwise I wouldn't be trying to tell my tale.

Outside you can hear the rain. Well not really the rain. You can hear the singing car tires as they rush by on the slick streets. Many people will die tonight. Today. Many but as I said before I don't want to get you overwhelmed that's why I'm just going to try and stay the course to our own little discourse. The few lives that are intersecting in this story. In case you're wondering though one hundred forty-seven thousand three hundred and thirty-three people died yesterday. The tally for today isn't in yet and tomorrow when Adrasteia dies will be different still. But for argument's sake that's around one and three quarters of a person dying per second. A few with each breath. But I'm not trying to be morbid. Most of these deaths are pleasant and of lives well lived. As it should be. Our examples in this story for the most part are about how not to do it. Sort of like reverse psychology if you will.

And on a day like today. A rainy night in New York City like tonight it is fitting that our story is perhaps a sad and melancholic tale. In a big city of so many people it is a fitting setting to find ourselves with our man Regin. His intense aloneness and loneliness like a constricting ice cold soaking wet straight jacket in a torrent of warm and abundant humanity. Even now as more people enter. An older couple celebrating their fiftieth wedding anniversary. A testament to fidelity and love. They will have ten more joyous years together. But even now with these myriad souls swirling around our man he might as well be alone on top of Mount Everest. Short of breath and cold to the bone. And as alone as the rock unblinking at the sun. Such intensity has his pain that he cannot be any more hollow and fragile.

So let us leave our fellow to drink in peace. To wallow in his pain for some time without our unblinking gaze. Let us move time forward to nine thirty this very same evening.

You'll hear a chime. Actually it is a melody and it goes on. It is his cell phone reminding him that it is nine thirty this evening. As it does every evening. Regin swallows the rest of his martini. It has been sitting there for some time. Armen comes by and he orders a whisky over ice. Our fellow lets the melody carry on. It is not unpleasant. It is Beethoven's Moonlight Sonata. There was a man who knew about loss but did not let it ruin him. Regin listens to the sobbing piano. It is hard to hear it. Not because it is so melancholic but because it is getting loud in here. In Bemelmans' at half past nine.

But this melody of Beethoven's might as well be plucked on the strings of our man's heart. Each plod of the piano like an ice pick in the heart. And he does this to himself every night at half past nine. And he thinks of Frea and Moana. He thinks of them in the subway smiling as when he saw them last. When he kissed them goodnight and they strode from the house. Both of them. The two women he loved the most turning and smiling and waving shyly goodbye. This is the image he has of them transplanted in the subway. This music the score of what is to come. But we must not rush this story. We must not rush our man Regin. He is feeling his heart squeeze and bleed. He is feeling his throat constrict. He feels the memories pour acid down his throat. He feels the memories burn like pepper in his eyes. And then he looks at his phone which he had before laid on the counter. It is now nine thirty-one. And he looks at the paintings of Madeline on the wall. And they left the house at half past nine he says. And that's all there is there isn't any more he says. And he grabs at the napkin to stanch the tears. He will not cry. He will be a brave soldier as his father admonished him. But I must interject here. Frea and Moana did not leave the house at half past nine. It was nine oh three. They died at half past nine on that train on their way to a show. But that is an aside. This is how we deal with the pain. This is how our fellow tries to cope. Yet he must be moving on now. Slowly for sure but steadily. And yet he is still as raw. Still as caught up in the catastrophe and it was a catastrophe to be sure as that day almost three months ago.

Zonah sees Regin mumbling to himself. She is smitten by this perceived vulnerability. She is thinking he must have had a bad day at the office. She will make this her opportunity. She catches Armen's attention. Can you see if he'll buy me a drink she says pointing to our man. I don't think that's such a good idea he says. He doesn't seem to be in a talkative mood Armen says. Will you try please she asks of him trying her best to be sultry. And she is young and she is used to getting her way with her female charms. Armen says okay sure but I warned you. He does it because he feels sorry for her. She seems like a sad and lost puppy. And as we know he is a good man this Armen. He will do well in this world. Well at the things that are important. Not the things that you think are important right now. So Armen walks over to our fellow and he is thinking that maybe these two. These lost souls need each other tonight. He is mistaken. It will ruin our fellow but it will turn out to be a salvation of sorts for Zonah. This is the sacrifice that will happen. These are the kinds of sacrifices I'd rather not see happen. Not like this. And this is why I tell this story. So that you will not have to suffer the sacrifices of others. So that you will not have to sacrifice yourself. I know I am redundant. You have no idea how important this is. Truly it is life and death and true salvation. To save yourself from difficult lessons. Horrendous exams. Trust me. Forgive me my redundancy. But it means that much to me.

And that's all there is there isn't any more our man says. Pardon me says Armen. He thinks our fellow is talking to him. Regin looks up from sleepy eyes. Though not really sleepy they just look that way. It is the alcohol. Nothing he says trying to smile but still unable. I was talking to myself he says. Sure says Armen as he leans in closer. Would you do me a favor please Armen asks. That young lady over there. And only his eyes gesture in her direction. That lady over there he says to our fellow asked me to ask you to buy her drink. I think she's lonely and I think she could probably use a drink he says. Our man looks over to see Zonah. She's looking at him coyly. She bites her lower lip and it does look vulnerable. It is quite sultry. Our fellow looks back at Armen. He doesn't say anything or gesture to her at all. Whatever she likes Armen he says. Thank you sir says Armen and he heads back towards Zonah thinking why is he getting caught in the middle of this. He thinks this is not right that our fellow is married. But he is mistaken. This is not right not because our fellow is mistakenly thought to be married but because he is about to ruin himself. Not to get me wrong. If our fellow was married this would not be right but for other reasons.

I must set this scene a little better for you I think. I sometimes forget you are not here with me to see to understand. Zonah is a nice looking woman. She is not beautiful but that is not her fault. That is the random role of the genetic die. It is not always the most handsome the most beautiful the smartest or the strongest sperm that gets to the egg with the same. Sometimes trust me it is pure chance. She knows that she is not model beautiful. So she overcompensates. She wears too much make up. Yet even without the overabundant makeup she would still have enough men interested in her. Because the package is quite nice. When you size up the whole one wouldn't be disappointed. Now don't get all high and mighty on me. I am not objectifying her. I am not objectifying women. But Zonah is here to be seen to be gawked at and to be desired by our man at the other end of the bar. So I am just setting the stage. This package if you will is well put together. When she left home which was in Uniontown Alabama she made her way to Birmingham the state's largest city. She worked there since she was sixteen at a diner and saved up her money until she could afford breast implants. Then closing in on her nineteenth birthday she figures she needed to come out here to New York. With some money not enough in her jeans and her firm breasts she comes here. Not necessarily a bad choice she just wasn't prepared and she was too naïve. That's now been taken care of. A hard lesson but well learned. Now she's broke and seeing our fellow as the answer. I'm rambling again. So she has a wonderful pair of breasts with ample cleavage that she is sharing with anyone who cares to look. And many do. Like two suns rising. She certainly has made the most of what she has been born with. It really is terrific. And she's in a short black leather skirt. The key word is short. If she bent over a pool table this would become a restricted story. Thankfully this is the type of establishment where you won't find a pool table. Her legs are bare. Not just shaved but barren of any stockings and her top is a deep red blouse. It would seem to come from the same cloth as our fellow's tie. Everything fits tightly. Snugly. And that is what Gier Vautour is thinking. He'd like to snuggle with her. Though his thoughts are more impure and I won't taint my story with them. But I'm sure you get the picture. Zonah is wearing FM boots. Fuck me boots if I can be so crude. They are knee high black leather with single zippers on the side. A good four inch high stiletto heel on each. Maybe more I didn't measure them. Her hair is golden locks cascading like a water fall midway down her back. Gier thinks of holding on to those locks like reins as he sees them both naked. But let us not get bogged down by Gier. He is like background noise at the symphony. Something to be ignored. Many men are admiring her this evening. Not our man. He is absorbed by his own pain. A blood-drenched blindfold if you will. But in time he will admire her. If only for a time. Zonah's skin is the color of roasted cashews. This is the Alabama sun for you. This gives her a glow of health. It carries the blood red of her blouse well. It matches those golden locks impeccably. This is the whole picture. A very nice portrait. I don't think I do her a disservice.

What will you have Armen asks. See I told you she replies smiling brightly. Happy with herself. Things are going as she had hoped. Listen says Armen I think he's married okay he's got a wedding ring. This is our decent Armen. A decent man. Not to worry says Zonah I can unmarry him. And she says this naively she does not mean to be flip. It is a lighthearted comment not to be taken seriously. What will you have Armen asks again. He has said his piece. He realizes he is not the ethics police. I'll have a Shirley Temple she says. Armen is surprised by this. He sees this as a lack of sophistication for a place like this. But she doesn't know any better. And besides who is anyone to judge. Shortly before Armen was thinking of carding her. She seems so young. But he doesn't. It is quiet in here and she is behaving herself. And in any event none of the customers seem to mind. Especially the men. So he goes to get her the cocktail. Zonah does not want her senses dulled. She wants to be at the top of her game. Sadly she has no game. She never played sports. Her parents never encouraged it. And they wouldn't have paid for it anyway. But she likes that saying. It gives her courage. Now that she has earlier had some liquid version of that. Courage that is. She looks over at our fellow and smiles at him. But he is not yet interested in her. He is not looking. He is mumbling to himself. It is inaudible. And that's all there is there isn't any more he says. And he says this many times over. And he thinks of the many times he has said that to Frea. Watching her fall asleep. Her little thumb no bigger than a jalapeno pepper as she sucks it. And then stops and then starts and stops again. And he sits and watches her. Watches sleep wash up all over her and drag her to the depths of peaceful dreaming. And he waits until she is fully asleep. And her eyes are swimming under her lids. And her thumb pops out of her mouth. He watches her then. So beautiful like an angel. Her hair golden too. Like Zonah's. And curly too. And he watches her breathe with her mouth slightly ajar. Then he leans in and kisses her on her head. And he can even now smell the apples in her hair from the shampoo. Even now he can feel that soft silkiness of her hair against his lips. And he puts the back of his hand against his lips in reverie. But it is not the same. And these memories vivid as they are are double edged swords. They keep him alive. But they also bring him to the brink of death. He thinks often of killing himself at times like these. He thinks of going home and shooting his brains out in her bedroom as he sits on her bed holding her bear Madeline. But when he gets home he cannot. He cannot do it. He is a coward. He is not the brave soldier his father admonished him to be. He is scared of losing these memories at death's hand. Even if they are painful. Even if they give him sleepless nights. For what else is there on the other side. The unknown is too scary. He cannot chance it. He cannot be a brave soldier. And this my friends is the twisted thinking that our man spars with. This is how we should not let loose the demons of our past to haunt and taunt us. We must be brave soldiers but in the true and honorable manner. Not allow the weakness of our forebears to impede upon what should be our own joyous journey. Live honestly and with integrity and joy and peace. The key here is honesty. Not like our fellow. He must be honest with himself before he can heal. Alas it is already too late. But not for us dear reader. Not for us who still slog it out each day. And it can be a slog. I won't deny you that.

But do not despair. Not everything need be despairing. All pain is surmountable. All pain is fleeting. All suffering is bearable. Life can be enjoyed. There is beauty and splendor and love abundantly if you will just look.

Again I get carried away. Zonah's smile is left to fall off her face. But she takes her drink from Armen as he frowns at her. A last attempt to change her mind. But her mind is made up. She takes the drink and sticks the straw in the side of her mouth. And she sucks it up. She enjoys the sweet tanginess. She gets up off the barstool and moves to the next one. Our fellow doesn't notice. He is in reverie. And I mean this truly. I mean that he is being delirious. From the old French rever. He is allowing delirium to ruin him and he will not stop himself. And this is his last night living. But he does not know that yet. We do. We can change things for ourselves. You and me. Together and singly. It can be done. It must be done. And I am certain that after this story friends it will be done. I believe in the human condition to become more than we are. To overcome great obstacles and still triumph. So Zonah sits on the barstool crossing her legs carefully at the knees. Showing him as much of her thigh as might be allowed by decency. In a place like this. And she is young. And you can imagine this thigh is very appetizing. It has not the cottage cheese of cellulite. This is the gift that is wasted on youth. Physical vibrancy. It is so carelessly deployed. Underappreciated. Our man once before "the incident" noticed the slow sagging of his skin. Around the belly and at the crease of his chest by his arms. He admired young men their vigor then. But he had it too as we all did. Do. But as I say it is a wasted gift on the youth. As much is. Sadly. But not on all of them. Some are as you say old souls. They are the ones living truly. This is what we need capture to do it right. To live without regrets so that outrageous fortune may not hurt us. May not wound our hearts and souls incurably.

Zonah has the straw stuck in the corner of her mouth. And she sucks intermittently on it. And Gier cannot help himself imagining her suck like that. But forgive me. Gier's static is interrupting us again. Zonah looks at our fellow. His eyes are closed. And that's all there is he says there isn't any more he says. And she thinks he is talking to her. That's okay mister I appreciate this drink. I don't want another. And now he opens his eyes and turns to look at her. And as he does he catches a whiff of her perfume. It is florally and fruity. He smells green apples. He thinks he sees Frea. But he is not that delirious. He is only mistaken for a split second. What was that he says to her not understanding what she is talking about. Oh I thought you were talking to me she says. I wanted to come and say thank you for the drink. They are close now. If she wanted to she could have her leg brush up against his. But she is trying to be coy. She is also a little nervous. You're welcome says our fellow and he turns back to the bar. He is drunk now. But not wasted. He turns to his whiskey and looks at it. And he thinks it is a similar color to Zonah's skin. But he is mistaken. It is darker. But he has noticed her now even though he doesn't know her name.

Zonah puts her hand on his knee. His left knee. She has nice slim fingers. Long and slender. The nails are blood red. Painted. He notices the warmth of her hand sink down to his flesh. And it prickles him. He hasn't felt the warmth of another human being. Not like this not for a few weeks. What is your name she asks him? And her heart is thumping a little harder now. Not only because of this new intimacy. But also because of the boldness of her gesture. This is quite new for her. This is also quite new for him. Regin he answers to his whiskey. And in it in the ice and the whiskey he can see a naked woman swimming around. And he knows already where this is going. He knows that he will soon provide a room here at this fine hotel for the two of them. And they will swim in the murky sea of sexual passion. And he thinks he will enjoy it. He thinks it will end his pain. But he is mistaken. It will ruin him. It will only give him momentary pleasure. And it will be fleeting. Like that first impression of heat. How it feels cold before it bites you. And this is what happened the last time. Sadly our good man will not learn. He will not try to help himself. He is not a brave soldier. Only because he believes it so.

I'm Zonah she says her hand still on his knee. Now it slides up just an inch. And as it does it feels like she has squeezed warm cream up our fellow's leg to his groin. This is how it feels. Hot and lusty. He enjoys it. He feels the warmth of it. The tickle all the way up his spine and then it pools in his groin. He looks at her. His eyes are heavy and sleepy. It is as if he has smoked opium all night. But it is the alcohol and the sexual tension. Zonah is looking deeply into his eyes. She is enjoying this sexual tension. It is part of her plan. Only things will not really work out how she would plan. But this is still to come. It is nice to meet you Zonah he says. That is a lovely name he says. And now for the first time this wet raining night he smiles. But it is a sad smile. A smile of longing and also of loss. It comes across the ages. Floats like fleeting mist upon the dark belly of a cold lake. But Zonah doesn't see it that way. For her he has taken the bait. This is the nod if you will. The nod and the wink. That understanding of desire. The baying dogs of sexual lust. Thank you she says. Your name reminds me of our old president she says. And she giggles. The pent up energy must be vented. I don't mean old she says but like from long ago she says. You know the guy she says. Regin is smiling. He is like a Cheshire cat now. He thinks he has caught a mouse. But it is a trap. A poisonous trap. Not set by Zonah but set by himself. He is tying his own noose around his neck. But he does not know it yet. Yes I know the guy our fellow says. Ronald Reagan he says. Yes that's it. She is still giggling and as she does her hand moves up another inch. More warmth floods our man's loins. He is getting an erection. He looks at her sucking her cocktail out of the corner of her mouth. Her lips as red as bright cherries. And he wants to bite them. He wants to have her now. This is our man losing control. Because he cannot dwell continually in the pain of his memories. And because the alcohol is diminishing his inhibitions. You know about that. This is our fellow seeking escape from the heat of the fire. This painful event. But doing it by jumping into the hearth. I am not exaggerating. You have no idea how he is flaying himself to death. Because he is making all the wrong choices. Let's count some of them now. The booze the women the dwelling the lonely brave soldier. These are all unhelpful. But he will not see it. In hindsight he will. Tonight he will. But much later.

So let us leave these love birds. These love birds in the cage of their own undoing. We will leave them to chat. To gaze into one another's eyes. To stimulate and whet the sexual appetite. And some men will be jealous and some women too. You know why. Because what they see is an apparition. It is their own interpreted illusion of the event. Not the real unraveling of a human life. This is what happens when you live in the shallows of life. Just because you are floating and don't touch the bottom does not mean you are in deep clear water. You are in the scum and muck of shallow existence. This is what happens when you dwell on the facile. When you abuse your physical existence by booze and drugs and unhealthy lifestyles. But now I am getting preachy. I do not mean to be preachy. I am just trying to show you. You will understand at the end. My passion will be forgiven.

Let us return then to this scene when we first met our fellow on his way to the bathroom. It is twelve oh five and our man empties his bladder. He gazes at the scoreboard. He enjoys the feeling of emptying his bladder. He feels anesthetized. All over his body is warm and tingling. He notices there is a small wet spot on his briefs. He has been sexually excited by Zonah. He sees them now fucking her naked body kneeling in front of him like a gift. Like an altar. And this is the word he uses in his own mind. He only ever made love to one woman. Her name was Moana. Zonah he will fuck. Because in his mind she is just a whore. He has lost all empathy having been wrapped up in his own angst. He has become too selfish. Zonah will be the second woman he will fuck since "the incident". I apologize if my crudeness is unnerving. I aim to be honest in my retelling. At least of the things that are important. And this is important because he is losing his humanity. He is objectifying this young woman. And yes she is looking for something from him too. But she has grown fond of him over these few hours. Dare she even think that there is the small bud of love bursting in her bosom. This is how she will be saved. She has her humanity. Her empathy and her honesty. Our fellow has lost it. And he will not look for it. And he will not believe that it is gone.

He washes his hands and rubs his face with them. He is getting his game face on. And he knows all about games. Of sports and competition. He returns back to Zonah and smiles at her. This smile is empty too. But not for Zonah. She is happy. Her dreams she thinks are coming true. This is sadly only gifted to the aged. The gift of wisdom. Of reading people honestly. This is a lesson that will take her several more years to master. Tonight she will just have a tiny sip of these bitter dregs. Shall we see what these rooms look like he says to her. And he winks at her. He is charming. He always was. Now he is using it insincerely. Yes please she says and she puts her hand through the crook in his elbow. What a lovely looking couple. What a lucky gentlemen some are thinking. What a slut some of the bitter women are thinking. Some though are just envious. Armen is disillusioned with the fragile foibles of humanity. But he sees this weekly. And each week he is rewarded by his own decency for he also sees the torrential river of the milk of human kindness. And this will be the teeter-totter that Armen will ride throughout life. And it

39

will be yours too if you get what my story is all about. But that will be okay. Because we are winning. More souls are escaping the harsher lessons than ever before. So you will be rewarded more than you are dismayed. Just don't lose hope. Be that beacon. That bright light in the choppy and rocky sea of life. Armen smiles to himself and vows to live honorably. In spite of what he sees here weekly. And he does and he will. And he also knows that he cannot judge too harshly. He has had to forgive himself of some unkindnesses along the way. He has not been perfect. But he has been honest. And this is the key. The key to salvation if I can say that. But let us not remain morbid about our fellow. All is not lost with him. Only this round. He has more rounds on his dance card of life. Hopefully he will learn sooner. Sooner rather than later. You who are blessed to hear of this now. Please learn the lessons now. It does not get easier. This here. This journey on earth is easy. Trust me. Easy compared to other travails. And our fellow will have other travails. And they will be considered torturous compared to this opportunity. From the Old French word trepalium. Three stakes. You can imagine. Enough said. Our love birds are moving through the foyer.

And we watch them as they walk. She has the walk of a model on the catwalk. She is tall too. She bobs a little above our man's six feet. She sashays as they say. Her hips rock and her buttocks roll. Our fellow will notice this later. He will be able to focus on other things rather than his interminable pain. If only for a short time. Although our fellow is drunk his prior athleticism will allow him to perform admirably tonight. Despite his waning years. And how soon the wick will extinguish. He has no idea. Yet despite these waning years the blood will flow easily to his extremities. And he walks with her.

And he can smell her perfume. He smells them apples and he grins. He does not see them looking at him. The other patrons. He is focused on his illusion. This illusion that he thinks will ease his pain. And he is mistaken. It will be the death of him. The yearning fragile growth of her. Previously he had obtained the key to the room. This is me being archaic. You know what I mean. He has the card to unlock the door to the room. And they climb into the elevator. Just the two of them. And as the doors close he turns to her and pulls her to him. They embrace and he feels her warmth. He tastes her lipstick. His tongue probes her mouth. It is wet and warm like maple syrup. She tastes of cherries and of sugar. This is the Shirley Temple from earlier. He tastes like burnt oak. But she does not mind. She is tasting the first blush of the blooming rose of mistaken love. And it is only mistaken because our fellow does not feel the same way. But she will find out soon enough. She is still naïve. And we hear the doors open. The ping of the elevator reminding them to behave. She giggles. She leans into his ear. I want you she says. He smiles. You have no idea he says. She giggles some more. They move down the hall to their room. She is bumping into him. He pulls her close by the waist. It is a slim waist and he likes it like that. He smacks her bum. It is taut. He feels his cock firming. Forgive me. I am only using the words he is using in his mind. In his mind he is thinking his cock wants her. She wants his cock. And this makes him smile. She sees him smile. But she does not see the blackness behind the smile. The internal misery like smog in his mind. She smiles back at him. Behind the smile he sees himself putting his cock in her mouth. But he is not a bad man. This fellow of ours. He is not mean-spirited. He is lost but he does not know it. He would not hurt her. He would not force her or even make her do anything uncomfortable. He is lost but thinks she is the signpost to salvation. He is mistaken. And if he was not lost. If he was not pained and wallowing in misery. This might work between him and Zonah. At another time and place. They might gel well. But he is like a man at night who cannot see. He thinks of himself as blind. But he is just lost. And Zonah is not a street lamp. She is an oncoming car that will hit him. And in a little while he will be ruined by this. So do not think too badly of our fellow. He means well but he is self-absorbed. And his soul in so much pain he thinks only the flesh can save him. But this is backwards. It is only his soul that can save the flesh. The soul does not grow weary. It is the flesh that is weak. But he is dishonest. He is avoiding the pain. And that is his mistake. He fumbles in his pocket for the cardkey. Zonah has her arms around his neck. She is kissing his cheek. He feels for the card and he finds his stiff member. He thrusts his hips at her. She can feel his member. Oooh she says. I think someone wants to play she says. You have no idea he says. He does not realize he is repeating himself. His mind is fogged up with booze and lust. This is a poor combination from which to make intelligent decisions. He takes the cardkey and opens the door. It is room eight one eight.

The room is nice inside. There is a king bed. Enough for Regin and for Zonah and for Frea and Moana. This is creepy. It is not meant to be. But Frea and Moana are aware of our man's difficulties. But they are helpless. Yet they yearn for him to do better. They are not here in a physical sense. Yet they are aware in the larger context. It comes back to being part of the whole. What happens to the one happens to the whole. You might think of it this way. When you tug at a corner of a sheet all the threads are affected. And this is how it works. This our man will learn. Zonah takes our man to the bed. She stands him just at the edge of it and turns on a bedside lamp. I am reminded of a moth attracted to a flame. I see our fellow the moth attracted to the flame that will extinguish him. Zonah is not the flame. His mind a mess is the flame. And this is where he will emolliate himself tonight. At this funeral pyre which he mistakes for the altar of lust. This has left him hollow before. Frea and Moana are aware of this. They want better for him. He knows this in hindsight. In the hindsight of the choking strangling Oxford around his neck. This comes later. We have seen this part already. The suffocating and choking and strangling. All because he chooses poorly. He would rather hide from the truth. He would rather cover it up and lie to himself. He will say to himself. He says to himself that he cannot manage this pain. But that is a lie. He can manage it. No it is not easy but it can be managed. It can become something from which to grow. It can soften him. Expand his soul. But he lies to himself. What will I do without them he thinks. But he is with them now as ever he was when they were physically present. This is true. Think about that. It is the larger context. Each thread attached to the whole. This he is blind to. This he will not see. He does not want to. He is not a brave soldier he thinks. This is also a lie. Metaphorically he is a brave soul. He can take this pain burn it up and birth a phoenix of himself out of the ashes. You know this is true. This is why I harp on the truth. As the wise man said. The truth will set you free. Always. Under all circumstances.

Alas I go off on my tangent. Let us rejoin Zonah and our fellow. Zonah is back now and she takes off his jacket and throws it across a chair. She takes off his tie and throws it on the chair. But it misses. It lies crumpled on the floor. I see it as a pool of blood. This is the blood being spilled tonight. Too much blood. She takes off his white shirt and tosses it towards the chair. It is lighter than the jacket and does not make it. It lands crumpled next to the tie. This is his white flag of surrender. This is his defeat. You might say he has stepped off the mine he was standing on. Now it will blow him up. He will not turn back now. Even though he could. She pulls off his undershirt and throws it away. He has no more flags of surrender. His briefs are blue. But we are not there yet. Mmm Zonah is cooing and our man is hard. Zonah is stroking his chest. He takes her to him and thrusts his cock at her. She feels his firm penis and she is wanting it. She wants to know what he feels like inside her. He just wants to fuck her. This is how he thinks. That is how she thinks. I'm going to fuck you he says. He thinks this is sexy. But really it isn't. Yet Zonah plays along with him. I want you to she says. And she slowly kneels down in front of him. She unbuckles his belt and tosses it aside. She rubs his penis through his slacks. It is hard and at eleven o'clock as she looks at it. Our man sees her kneeling at his feet. He sees her worshipping at his cock. This is how he gets his pleasure. He cannot see her as Moana's equal even though she is a woman. He could not do this without sullying her. Himself really. But remember. He is not a bad man. He is not mean-spirited. If you will these are two lost souls colliding in chaos. This is not how it should be. It should be more honest. More thoughtful. Zonah pulls down his pants and helps him step out of them. He is in stocking feet and briefs. She can see a wet spot through his briefs. She is pleased with this. He wants her she thinks. But this does not mean he loves her. This is her error. She will learn in time. Our fellow is standing before her. He pats her head. It is awkward. He is thinking how she wants to suck his cock. How she wants to taste his cum and worship at his altar. But this is awkward. Because his thoughts are disingenuous. He does not believe them fully. But this is what he needs. This is our good man's attempt at salvation. She takes his briefs off and his penis lurches at her like a pointing finger. This is not what she thinks. It is wagging at her. Naughty naughty it could be saying. Because she is not seeing the honest picture. She thinks there is more to this than simple sex. This is her mistake. She mistakes this wagging finger of his as his desire for her. A.k.a. his love for her. This is her mistake. Oh yeah baby he says. Put my cock in your mouth he says. She looks up at him. Like this she says as she encloses his penis in her mouth. The end tastes salty. Ahhh our man says. This is what he has been waiting for. He groans some more and looks down at her. She is looking up at him. He likes what he sees. She joined to him by her mouth. She bobs up and down the length of his cock and she is making cooing sounds. He is thinking how much she likes to suck his cock. She is just wanting to please him because she is mistaken. She thinks this pleasure is his reward for his love and devotion to her. She takes her mouth off his penis and strokes it with her hand. It is glistening now. From her saliva. She sees a small drop of clear cum squeeze out of the end. This is like tears. Like the tears he cannot cry. Mmm she says. I like that she says. Somebody is enjoying this she says. Yes baby he says. Taste me he says. And she flicks her tongue across the head to catch it. Mmm very nice she says. But she exaggerates. She takes his cock back in her mouth and he thinks he will choke her with it. He takes her head in both his hands and rocks his hips towards her. But he is gentle. He is not a bad man. He is lost. But this focus is steadying him. He feels nothing. But at least the pain has subsided. But the pain is always there. It is just hiding. But it will not hide for long. It does not like to hide. It is not the place for turmoil and pain to be hidden. They will come back with a vengeance. And they will come back with their rowdy friends. This is guilt and low self-esteem. They will team up on him and beat him down. Because he would not deal with the pain and burn it up. Use it to fuel the rest of his journey until his true time is up. Not this aborted attempt at leaving the pain behind. This will not do. This is the coward's way out. This is our fellow not being a brave soldier. Because he is not honest. Because he does not believe in himself. And by not believing in himself he does not believe in humanity. This is a grave error.

He looks down at her. She is enjoying his cock he thinks. I will bless her with my cum he thinks. She is thinking I will take his penis inside me soon. These two people on very different pages. That feels so good he says. I like to watch you sucking me he says. She is busy. Her mouth is full. It is as if he is a dentist trying to talk to her. But she hums in answer. She takes his penis out of her mouth and rubs it. Licking the tiny drops of cum that squeeze from the tip. Perhaps this is his soul's way of crying. For soon he will be in anguish. More lonely than he was a few hours ago at the bar by himself.

He lifts her up off the floor and takes her clothes off. They puddle more neatly by her feet. And this is like the human body. At the end of the journey it will lie like a puddle. Of no more use. But don't be mistaken. It must be nurtured and valued while alive. Not like these two are doing. They are sullying the flesh and it rubs the soul wrong. It bruises the soul. This disrespecting of the body. But let us get back to where we were. He enjoys her red bra and thong. He pulls them off and puts her onto the bed with her legs resting on his shoulders. She is open to him as he stands before her. He puts his cock inside her. He enjoys that first thrust. The warmth and the tightness of it. Not that he is extremely large. It is just that she has not had him before. And she is young. She has not birthed children. She will one day. A boy and a girl. And the boy will be named Regin. A nice gesture. A gesture of longing and melancholy over this night. And perhaps what could have been. But that is not where our story is going. We must stay the course. We are with our fellow. He is fucking Zonah. She is moaning and cooing. He is watching his cock stab her. In and out. I like to see me inside you he says. She moans at this. I like the way you feel inside me she says. These are strangers really. Strangers intimately connecting in the most physical way. It is awkward. That is how it is. These things are not to be rushed. It can create difficulties. Honesty and trust come to mind. He can feel the pressure build. In his cock. He pulls himself out of her and turns her over on all fours. I want to fuck you from behind he says. Like a bitch he thinks. And she obliges. And he goes to work. He reaches around her back and grabs at her breasts. He likes them. Soft but firm. This is the gift of youth. He is abusing this gift of youth. This position is awkward. He grabs her at the waist and he drives himself hard into her. He hits her buttocks. She groans. It is not very hard. It is the sentiment. She is close to orgasm. He feels thick and warm inside her. She likes it. She is falling in love with him. This is her giving herself to him. Because she thinks he is falling in love with her. He is about to orgasm too. You want my cum baby he says. Yes she says. Ahhh she says. My god I'm coming too. He feels the pressure build inside of him. He feels the release as he squirts himself inside her. My god you're making me cum he says. And he clutches her strongly around the waist. She is moaning. I love you she says quietly. But he does not hear her. His orgasm is in full play. He feels his life deflating like a balloon as he cums inside her. Oh Moana he says. And he does not stop himself. It is too late. She hears this and her world comes crashing in around her. But she does not understand. They are finished now. He retreats and lies exhausted on the bed. She is aware of her awkwardness now. Her nakedness. She feels like Eve. She has just eaten the apple. She is aware of her sin. But this is not really sin. This is lying and being found out. This is the dawning of truth. The heat of honesty. This is what she feels. It may masquerade as shame or sin. But it is the blinking awakening eye of honesty. He feels it now and it sucks out the brashness and lust and weakness of the flesh. It leaves him hollow. It leaves her hollow. This is not the melding of souls. It was the banging of flesh. And flesh is just a wine skin. It is the soul inside that must be respected. Protected. But it is not. The flesh like hollow wine skin is not protecting the soul. It is getting battered and bruised by this banging. This coarse sex. This mistaking lust for connection. Physical intimacy for the deeper longing of the soul. The soul of one seeking to acknowledge the soul of the other. But this they have not done. This has been the mind abusing the body for power. Bruising the soul. And this is the hollowness felt deep inside. The poverty. They are both aware of it now. This is not honesty. Not to oneself and not to the other.

She crawls under the sheet and turns to face the lamp. She is sad and confused. But she shouldn't be. She will understand. This is a lesson learned. And not a very harsh one. She feels his seed leak out of her. No longer does it feel as good. It is slimy now between her legs. Like snot. And this is how she thinks. She thought it was more. But how could it have been. They don't even know each other. Our fellow lies on his side outside of the covers. He is naked. Except for stocking feet. He thinks he must look like an idiot. How right he is. His cock is now a drunken soldier fallen down. No longer brave. An imbecile that must rest on the grassy knoll. Our man puts his arm above his head. He is looking at the ceiling but there is not much to see. Fuck he thinks to himself. She is lying still as death next to him. A statue. She does not breathe or move. This is how it looks. This is how awkward it is. The dawning of truth. The xenon light of realization. His mind is now too small a cage for his thoughts. He turns to her and puts his hand on her shoulder. I'm sorry he says. He does not rub her back. This is the best he can do. It's and he pauses. He does not want to get into it. But this is our man. And he is not a bad man. He is lost. It's he says again. My wife he says she died just a couple of months ago. And then he stops. Silence walks into the room. He is a looming figure big and dark and he sits himself down. And he stares at them. And he waits. Someone will acknowledge him. They always do. He's too big a presence to be ignored. But seconds go by and they feel as large as elephants. Our fellow. The good fellow is the first one to see silence. That was her name he says. I just miss her he says. And as if she were here listening quietly. Moana hears. But if Zonah were listening quietly she would hear that first scratch in his voice. Like the scratch of diamonds on glass. It is his voice almost cracking. But at this game he will be a brave soldier. He will not show his fragile self. He will not crack. But this is a lie. He is broken already. He has been smashed into a million pieces. But they are beautiful pieces. And if he could just acknowledge it. If he could just accept the truth. Let it be with him. Let this pain out of its cage. He would not be scared anymore. He would not be alone and lonely. And he could build himself up. From these millions of beautiful pieces. And all the cracks would shine brilliant rainbows and he would be more than he was. If he could only allow himself some honesty. If he could only be the brave soldier that he thinks he isn't. But he could do it. I want to tell you that. You can do it too. This is the gift of the soul. Part of being of the whole. It is the manifest destiny. And this is not a hardship. It is not insurmountable. Not with honesty. Not with courage and vigilance. Not with integrity and valor. It can be done. Our friend doesn't. He won't allow himself. He sees these truths as copouts. But they are the way to salvation. Not blind alleys. He is in a blind alley. This is his mistake. It doesn't have to be yours. She turns to him then and smiles at him. Her eyes are kind. He sees this and he feels worse. He shouldn't. Okay she says. I'm sorry too she says. The bartender told me you were married she says. He shakes his head. I was he says but I don't like to talk about it. He is trying a smile but he is not successful. I really like you she says. I was hoping this was going somewhere. She stops then scared of the answer. She bites her lower lip. This is unconscious. She looks at a corner of the pillow his head is resting on. She twirls her hair with her finger and waits. Silence shuffles in his seat. I like you too he says. Maybe it can go somewhere he says. Maybe I can buy you dinner sometime he says. These are not truths. These are wishes. Secret passages to escape from the awkwardness. Though he means well. He wouldn't be in this predicament if he had been up front with her. Even if he had just told her from the beginning all he wanted was sex. Then this might have been better. Less awkward. Not without misgivings but less so than this. I'd like that she says. Good he says and he gets up. Why don't you get some sleep he says and we'll order breakfast in bed in the morning. I'm going to go have a shower. His head is wooly. He is not making any sense to himself anymore. He feels lost in quicksand and this is his attempt to get out. He leans in and kisses her on the forehead. She smiles and closes her eyes. I am a shit he is thinking to himself. And instead of allowing himself this error. This mistake. Instead of allowing his flesh this weakness. Instead of accepting his stumble he sees it as a fall into oblivion. But it is not. Even now he could still recover. These have not been grave errors. Mistakes certainly. But not grave errors. He who is weak. Our man will not allow himself this weakness. He thinks by doing this he is being a brave soldier. But he is not. It is the weakness. His vulnerability that he must embrace. It will hold him up. It will support his new growth. And he will come out the other side cracked and splintered. But this is where the light comes out dazzling as a rainbow. He does not see it this way. This is sad. Sad and morbid. Morbid because he now knows better. We all do. Through this story. But we must get back to our fellow. Follow him into the bathroom where he takes a shower. Hot and it makes his skin pink. He is trying to burn and wash off the stain that he thinks he wears. But he wears no such thing. Without honesty he feels confused. It is honesty that he needs to embrace. Acknowledge his failings and his vulnerabilities. This is how it is to be human. Vulnerable and scared sometimes and lonely. But seeing the truth of this is the way out of the blind alley. He could find his way again. This honesty. This acceptance of sadness and vulnerability and hurt could heal him. Truth could be his compass. Guide him to healing. Build up those millions of pieces into brilliance and he could shine anew and be stronger. But he is missing the links. This he does not do. This investigating of the truth. And so he is like a beached whale. The sonar has been hijacked. And so he steams himself in the shower and still it does not help. He needs fresh air. He needs space he is thinking. But he can't escape himself. This longing for air and space is a longing for the truth. Again he is misguided as to the answer. He dries himself off and climbs into his clothes. He looks at Zonah. She is sleeping peacefully. The light is muted in the room. Zonah's mouth is slightly ajar and he sees Frea sleeping peacefully many years ago. That's all there is there isn't any more he says quietly under his breath. This sight increases his pain. Not because he thinks he is looking at the woman he just fucked as his daughter. But rather the innocence on her face like Frea is knife in his heart. He must embrace this pain. This is his love and longing for his family. It is to be allowed. But he doesn't know what to do with it. He needs to acknowledge it truthfully. Allow it room to escape. Through tears. Through dialogue and through journeying with the pain to its destination. But he can't do that. He thinks he needs to be a brave soldier. But this stiff upper lip routine is killing him. He will realize this in hindsight when it is too late. He leaves the room but as he does he turns to look at her one last time. Zonah in the muted light. Frea in his muted memories. He is determined to return in time and have breakfast with her. Acknowledge that he can't continue this with her in his current state. This would be his first step towards honesty. But that doesn't happen. We know why. But it would have been a good start. He leaves the hotel and collects his car. He is in no state to drive. Not emotionally and not legally. It is twelve fifty am on Thursday morning. In ten minutes Adrasteia will be dead. This is how the story unfolds. Unknown to both of them at this time. And it happens primarily because our fellow won't embrace the truth and needs fresh air. He needs honesty is what he needs. And for the wanting of a little honesty and understanding of the self and of others we are coming to the end of this domino effect. Two people will die at our fellow's hands tonight. Adrasteia and himself. This is unnecessary and this is the thrust of my story to you. The way it could be different. The opportunities you will have. So as our fellow waits for his car let us join Adrasteia.

She is with her boyfriend Atlas. And this is a fitting name. He will endure this loss better than our man has. He will hold the memory of her up like the heavens giving honor to it. But he will live his life fully because he will explore the pain and be its traveling companion until it departs him. This is the only way. But this is not the story I am telling. That would be too easy and perhaps it would fall on deaf ears. It is only in the retelling of this difficult and sorrowful tale that I believe the true effect can be permanently felt. I must give you some background on Adrasteia to enable you to empathize. These are keys in the tale of morality if you will. Empathy and honesty. With these keys you can unlock the gates to salvation. And of course the golden rule. But that should go without saying. Adrasteia is also nineteen years old. She and Atlas have been dating since they were thirteen. Real childhood sweethearts. Two months ago they became engaged but planning for a long engagement. Enough time for them to finish college. Adrasteia was going into nursing. Atlas was enrolled to start in mechanical engineering. He finishes his degree and designs the 'cocoon'. It is used to protect occupants of motor vehicle crashes in ten years time. It will save countless lives. Estimates suggest over fifty percent fewer deaths since the introduction of the cocoon when it comes out. This is how he honors her and his own growth through the pain. This is how it can be done. Our fellow could have chosen a path along those lines. But he doesn't and we're starting to see the results. But we're also tasting different paths that could be taken. My biggest hope is that you will be able to take the better paths. So we are with Adrasteia. She is at the door of her car. Atlas has walked her out. The rain has stopped for now. But the roads are slick and wet. Atlas and Adrasteia have just finished watching a movie at his parents' house. They are embracing. They recently returned from four months in Europe and India. It was their pre-honeymoon they called it. Atlas lives down in Soho so does our man. He is subconsciously driving back home. I love you says Atlas. I love you too honey she says. I can't wait for school to start in the fall she says. Yeah I know he says then we'll be closer to getting married. She likes to hear him talk like this. He is honest. He is looking forward to their lives together. Drive safe my love he says to her. The roads look slick he says. I will she says but I'm sleepy. It's not you I'm worried about he says. She kisses him on the lips. I'll be careful she says and she is careful. But what is to come is not her fault. Text me when you get home he says I'll be waiting up. She is on her way to her parents' home in Queens. I will she says and she gets in to her little car. It is a subcompact. This doesn't help but it is all she can afford. It is also ten years old. This also will not help in the accident to come. Atlas closes her door and watches her drive off. He kisses his fingers and waves off after her. There is a big smile on his face. He has found his love. And he sees her wave back at him. This is the last time he will see her until the funeral. But he will have no regrets with this parting. She knew he loved her. He knew she loved him. No moments between them were wasted even just sitting down on the couch watching a movie together. The pain will seem unbearable at times. But he will overcome. He lived with empathy and decency and honesty and he treated people as he wanted to be treated. It's that easy.

He watches her drive down the road. On his face is a big smile. He is a handsome ruggedly good looking man. He sees her flash her hazards at him. Atlas turns around and walks back into his parents' house. Right now at this moment his life is grand. That will change in three minutes and twenty seven seconds. But he will not know about it for another hour. You know how it goes. The next of kin are notified first. And Atlas is not next of kin.

But this is not a story about Atlas. It is not even a story about Adrasteia. It is a story about our man Regin. Regin Sigurd. Our man has climbed into his car and he is driving towards destiny. I say that but it is not quite true. This is his destiny only because he has made these poor choices. He could have chosen otherwise. But he does not know that he is driving towards destiny. He is inebriated. We know that. But that is not the only reason he should not be driving. He is also an emotional wreck. Regin is driving through a thick fog of his own pain and pooling tears. Two straight lines he says as he starts to weave in and out of traffic. Two straight lines he says again as he speeds up and runs right through a deeply orange traffic light. Two straight lines that pierce my heart he says. He is not here in the now. He is at home with his young daughter. He is reading her a bedtime story. It was always Madeline that Frea wanted and he had bought them all. She is cuddled up under his arm. She has her thumb in her mouth and she is looking intently at the pictures. For one Halloween when she was nine Moana made her a costume so that she could look like Madeline. Only a few of the adults figured it out as they went from house to house. Frea loved her yellow hat with the two black tassels.

Traffic is light at one minute to one on this unfortunate morning. Perhaps if it had been busier Adrasteia might not have died. But the die was cast a long time ago. We might say the die had been cast almost two decades ago. But that would only be partially correct. If we are going that far back we might say the die had been cast at Regin's birth. But these things are hard to determine absolutely. You see there are always choices. And these choices we make from microsecond to microsecond reverberate across the universe. Literally changing destinies. Even now as we watch our man driving towards Adrasteia with thirty seconds left on the clock there are choices being made that could change things still. But he won't make these choices. He won't open his eyes to the honesty. Instead he prefers to drive towards his own demise. They left the house at half past nine he says. Half past nine and blown apart by a deathly mine he says. He is becoming more morbid. That's all there is he says. There isn't anymore he says.

Adrasteia is driving along minding her own business. She doesn't have too long to get home. You might think she is already halfway there. The light is green as she travels through it slightly below the legal speed limit. Adrasteia is listening to the radio and she has the window open slightly to help keep her awake. The station is one of these mainstream top of the pops. None of this is important. Our man Regin brings his forearm up to his face to staunch the pooling tears in his eyes. He is trying his best to be a brave soldier. But brave soldiers don't kill innocent civilians. His eyes are blurry from the tears and the booze. He does not notice that the light is already red when he is almost upon it. He has been speeding up. This is also his error. He does not notice that he is well past sixty miles an hour. In fact he is doing exactly sixty-six miles an hour when he slams into the driver's side of Adrasteia's car. If there is any small kindness it is this. She is dead instantly. Well I should say almost. What would be more accurate is to say that she is dead quickly without knowing what happened. Perhaps that is a small kindness. I'll let you be the judge of that.

As often happens the drunks get off scot-free in situations like this. Most of the time. Regin was wearing his seat belt and the airbag went off. His BMW also has the best safety features. Our man stumbles out of the car. He is dazed and confused. He is also not quite sure what just happened. He staggers around. He combs his fingers through his hair. Jesus he says. Jesus he says again. He stumbles up to Adrasteia. He looks into the car. There is blood everywhere. Adrasteia is dead already. She has a big gash on the side of her head. Jesus our man says. Fuck no he says. No no no he says. Our man Regin is full of bad decisions. He is stuffed full of them. He is like a teddy bear with its side open and the stuffing pouring out. The stuffing is Regin's bad decisions. He looks around. The pavement is wet and he starts to run. He stumbles and almost falls. Regin knows he is blitzed. He knows this will not end well for him. He wants to escape. He wants to escape everything. He is like the insane in a padded room. This padded room is his body. He wants to escape it all. But he can't. There are consequences. You know this. Navarum Nanshe knows this. He is out with friends just having finished a shwarma at a local restaurant. They are walking down the sidewalk when they see the accident. Navarum Nanshe Nansh to his friends is first on the scene. He is young. Twenty-seven. He easily catches up with Regin and stops him from running away. Regin gives no fight. Our man is easily led back by Navarum to the sidewalk where he is seated. Navarum stands over him and watches until the police arrive. They arrive quickly. Within three minutes from the first call. This call came from Shala Adad. She owns the shwarma shop. What did I do says Regin. Navarum looks down at him. He feels a mixture of anger and pity. Regin is not looking at him. He is talking to the ground as he leans his head on his hands. It is one oh two in the morning. You can hear the sirens now like fighting cats getting louder and louder. In less than ninety minutes our man will be dead. He does not know this yet. Now he is a tight mass of pain and confusion. I've killed my daughter he says. Navarum frowns. He does not know if this is true or not. It is not true. But Regin can be forgiven for thinking that Adrasteia is his daughter. She is the same age. And in this dark night with blood all over her face Adrasteia reminds him of his daughter. But he is mistaken. He is confused and he is in shock and inebriated.

But we'll leave our man here. At the side of the road. As he rocks back and forth mumbling to himself. We know where this goes now. Don't we? We met him with his shirt around his neck. Already dead. That was how this story started. The police come and they lock him up. He takes his own life. There is a lesson there. Is there not? He is stuffed full of bad decisions. This is our man Regin. And he could have made better choices. But I am being too hard on our man you say. I am not. I am not angry or filled with bitterness. Au contraire gentle reader. I am merely the teller of a tale. A tale of tragedy and of sorrow. But we must move along. I must offer you further glimpses into the life of our man Regin. Then you will see that over the years he had ample opportunity to make different choices. It was his choices that got him here in the first place. Let his life be a warning sign along your own journey. That is my hope. And like all of our tales Regin's is not solely morbid. We will see the love and joy that was abundant too. But it's the choices. The choices that lead us to our destiny. And from such a sorrowful chapter we must now turn to another. Let us travel back now to a Sunday. A Bloody Sunday.

The Middle

It is the thirtieth of January. It is a Sunday. A Sunday that will become another Bloody Sunday. Those astute students of world history will be aware of at least one other Bloody Sunday. The Bloody Sunday that affected those in Northern Ireland in nineteen seventy-two. But this is not a history lesson. No not directly. This is a tale of our man Regin. It just so happens that the thirtieth of January is also a Sunday. And it too will become another Bloody Sunday. Picture this. We are in a Manhattan apartment. It is a large apartment. Over two thousand square feet. It is worth several million. This was one of the good decisions that Regin made. He bought it for three point three million. He has easily doubled his money. He takes great pride in this. And well he should. Some of you my dear readers might find it difficult to empathize with a millionaire. What one now calls the one percent. I can understand that. But do not think of this as the banal troubles of the very rich. The key theme here. Which I'll harp on again and again is the choices. There is a theme of bad choices. Not very many. But enough that ruin a man's life. It is the how of living that we are interested. Not the accouterments of living. This story is applicable to those in destitute poverty to those in the point one percent bracket. But before we carry on let us talk a little about our man's wealth. How he got it. How relevant might it be to us. Regin is a rich man. According to some figures he would be in the point one percenters. The actual numbers are not important. But suffice it to say his wealth is over twenty million. A tidy sum. Regin would call himself a self-made man. That is wholly inaccurate. As is much of what the one percenters think. It is true he came from humble means. His father was a janitor and his mother cleaned houses. There were four kids and he was the only one who went to college. He worked hard. I won't deny him that. He got scholarships. He worked two jobs in the summers and one during the semesters. He worked for the same company for twenty-five years. For the last three years he's the CEO. He stepped down recently. As you can imagine. He steps down in just a few days from today. For personal time. But what he doesn't understand is all the people that work hard to help him achieve what he has. He is not an island unto himself. But he thinks he is. This is also his error. This is the fatal error of belief of the one percent. Perhaps what is worse if I can be preachy is Regin's success. He holds himself up as an example of the American dream. Society holds him up as an example of the American dream. But much of his success is luck. The luck started when he was three. When his parents brought him over from the old country. He got lucky with the love and support he received from his parents. He got lucky with mentors in college. He got lucky with getting the jobs he's had. It is not all based strictly upon merit. He got lucky in moving up the ranks. An example. When he was Vice President of International Operations the CEO dropped dead of a heart attack. The man was in his early fifties. Regin's position was high profile and the international markets were on his fire. This was without his help either. Just the way the global economy was humming along. He got pinned for the big gig. Nevertheless there are those of you who will prefer to disbelieve. That is not my concern. I'm on a tangent in any case. But this idea of the American dream being alive and kicking. Well that's just incorrect. That's the hope opium you've been smoking. The American dream is a trampled cadaver in the gutter of wishes and dreams. You wouldn't recognize him anyhow. But I digress. There is a way to resurrect it but that is another tale for another time. Suffice it to say it requires egalitarianism and social equality. But we'll not get into that now. We need to look into our man Regin. He's at the dinner table with his wife and daughter. You remember them. Moana and Frea respectively. We've heard snippets about them before. We'll get to know them well as we travel along this tale. Moana is in the kitchen just finishing up dinner. She is a marvelous cook. Frea and Regin sit at the table. Between them is a big bowl of salad. It contains mixed greens slivered almonds avocado sweet onion tomatoes croutons and a honey vinaigrette. They eat well in the Regin household. Regin looks at his daughter and smiles. She reminds him of his wife when they first met. And it is true. They could be sisters. Though of course Moana is thirty-one years older. She is tall for a woman. Five foot ten. She has long straight blond hair and high cheek bones. You would assume she modeled when she was younger. That assumption would be accurate. She has kept herself attractive and slim all these years. Men notice her and women are envious. But as you know our man Regin is no slouch either. He is tall and athletic. Handsome in a rugged way. Those within their sphere of influence remark at each other that they're the perfect American family. And they look like it too. Regin Moana and Frea. You'd see them in advertisements for Aspen. Good looking people. They present well and they symbolize the realization of the American dream. But we won't get into that again. Their home life is blissful. Regin and Moana very seldom share a sharp word. And they're doting parents. Frea has never wanted for anything. She sits next to her father. They both wait for Moana to serve them up. Moana has made Shepherd's Pie. On the side is pan fried asparagus. Moana brings in the dishes. Regin has the largest serving. But Moana has not been shy with hers or Frea's. Regin pours red wine from a bottle on the table. He pours for Moana first. Then Frea. Then himself. He lifts his glass and Moana and Frea lift theirs. To my beautiful stars in my sky he says. They clink glasses. Thank you for dinner my love he says. Moana smiles at him. Thanks Mom says Frea. My pleasure says Moana. Steam dances seductively from the Shepherd's Pie like a sultry belly dancer. Our man spears an asparagus with his fork. What Regin doesn't realize is that there is no beef in this Shepherd's Pie. Moana is vegetarian. So is Frea. She has made the pie with vegetarian beef. They have eaten this meal before. It is one of their favorites. In the past Moana assured our man that she made his separate with real beef. But she does not. It is because she cares for him. His doctor is concerned about his cholesterol. His one vice is a weekly steak. Moana cooks it for him. It is delicious but it is small. Only six ounces. It used to be eight. But that was before his cholesterol worsened. Now he only gets meat twice a week at home. The rest of the evening meals are prepared with either chicken or fish. Moana is doing her best to take care of her husband's health. But she is being undermined. Our man Regin is undermining her. As I've said before. He is stuffed full of bad decisions. His doctor has told him to cut back. But three and sometimes four times a week he dines at a steakhouse for lunch. Moana is unaware of this. On these occasions he eats twelve ounce steaks. This is our man being self centered. Behaving like a petulant schoolboy. This is our captain of industry who thinks he knows better than anyone else. But he loves his family. You can see it in his eyes. As he looks around from his wife to his daughter. What an elegant young woman Frea has become. Frea is in her second year at Juilliard. She is a dance major. On the side she earns money modeling. She is level headed and smart. Tonight at half past nine she will leave Demetrios Epimetheus behind for good. This is because she dies. This is not done purposefully. Demetrios is her beloved. His family is Greek and he is a good young man. They most likely would have gotten married. Demetrios does not take her death well. He goes into a major depression which he does not come out of for one year. And then the recovery is slow. It will take him three years to get back to where he was. And where he is right now is a Junior at Columbia. But this is not about Demetrios. It is not really about Frea. Or Moana. It is about our man Regin. He sits and eats dinner with his wife and his daughter. He tosses salt onto his Shepherd's Pie. He grinds pepper onto its white face. He drinks his red wine. He puts a forkful of pie into his mouth. It is savory and delicious. He thinks he tastes the beef. But he is mistaken. He looks at Frea. There was an article in today's paper he says that had good things to say about the play. Frea nods. I remember reading it in high school she says. It's quite tragic says Moana. More like a fairytale says Regin grinning. Why do you say that asks Moana. Because Willy Loman was a lunatic who never amounted to anything says Regin. In this country if you work hard continues our man you can become successful. As such it is a fairytale he says. Perhaps says Moana but I think it more accurately portrays the disillusion and difficulties that some have in achieving the American dream. It's just a play says Regin. Yes father says Frea but one of the greatest plays of the twentieth century. Well I'm just glad that you and your mother are going out to have a fun evening he says.

Our man looks at his watch. It is just after eight in the evening. When are you leaving asks Regin. Moana takes a moment to finish eating a mouthful of food. We thought we'd leave just after nine she says. But it only starts at ten doesn't it he says. Moana nods her head. It does she says. But we want to get there with time to spare she says. You never know she says. We might want to do a bit of shopping beforehand. Of course says our man. How foolish of me he says. He grins at her and she smiles back at him warmly. We promise not to spend all your money Daddy says Frea. He likes that. He likes it when she calls him Daddy. Better than father or dad. Just the same way she used to call him when she was small. Only now her voice has matured. She is a woman. And as he looks at her he is puffed up with pride. Our man Regin loves his family. He is in a position of envy. He is a lucky man and he knows it. But the destruction of his family is the destruction of himself.

They continue to eat dinner and drink wine. On a side plate Regin puts salad. He eats some salad and then he eats some Shepherd's Pie. Then he eats some asparagus. Our man watches his daughter spear asparagus and pile on some Shepherd's Pie. He does not know where she gets this from. Both he and Moana like to eat each food group by itself. Never shall the twain mix he says to himself. But Frea prefers to combine her food. She enjoys the taste of the flavors mingling. Not Regin and not Moana. Though Moana is not as adamant about it as Regin is.

You've always liked to mix your food haven't you darling asks Regin. Frea looks up at her father. At first she is not sure if he is talking to her or to her mother. She realizes he is talking to her. She nods her head and chews her food. I like to see how the flavors mingle and complement each other she says. Regin smiles and nods at her. And yet neither your mother nor I do that he says. Moana looks over at him. Though I'm not as stringent about it as you she says grinning at him. He looks over at her and winks. I am allowed to be my own person says Frea cheekily. Of course says Regin. He eats some salad. And when it is swallowed he drinks some wine. He looks out the window at the black sky. It is not fully dark. It never is in New York City. Street lamps smear the air with nicotine light. Large flakes of snow lend a thickness and weight to the air.

You sure you don't want to take the car he asks looking at Moana. Moana nods. I could drive you too he offers. Moana shakes her head. That's not necessary my love she says. I don't want any of us to have to risk driving out in conditions like this she says. The subway will be safer and warm she says. Regin looks over at Frea to see if he can win her onto his side. He can't. Frea nods her head and smiles at her father. I agree with Mom she says. No need to take any more risk than necessary she says. Frea has always been conservative. She has never been one to take much risk. She has always followed the tried and true path. She wouldn't even go on the roller coaster rides at Disneyland. Even when she was small she was cautious. Regin has come to admire that. Especially as she grew into a woman. He never once worried about her being out late. She always held to her curfew. Never slept around or worried him with pregnancy. To be transparent. Frea is waiting until marriage to give herself to Demetrios. Not that they don't fool around. They do other things. But those things are not relevant to this tale. Suffice it to say that Regin has not shared in the fears of most other fathers of daughters.

Our man picks at the Shepherd's Pie. There are more tomatoes and perhaps beans than beef in it. You did use real beef in this he asks. Moana looks over at him briefly. In yours yes she says. Do you not like it she asks. No no he says. It is delicious he says. Just doesn't seem to be much meat in it he says. There isn't says Moana as she puts a serving of the Shepherd's Pie on her fork. You know what your doctor says she says. Regin looks up at her like a scolded schoolboy. He grins. Doctors just don't want me to have any fun he says. Moana doesn't look at him. Well I'd rather you not have fun and stick around with us for a long time than not be here she says. Then she looks over at him and grins. It's for your own good darling she says.

My own good repeats our man. What good is it if life is devoid of pleasure he says. Well says Moana we could always become vegan. She looks at him and offers a wry smile. He chuckles under his breath. Not in this lifetime he says. Well Frea and I have been thinking about it she says. It's very healthy she says. That's sacrilegious he says. Keep your voice down he chides. The neighbor's might hear he says. He smiles at her with a wicked gleam in his eye.

You're being silly Daddy says Frea. Mom and I have been looking into it and it would do your heart the world of good she says. What she doesn't know is that within the hour there is nothing that will do Regin's heart any good. Not when the news comes. We'll see what the doctor says about my cholesterol next time I see him says Regin. You realize that Mommy has never had a cholesterol problem says Frea. Regin looks at his daughter as he gets lectured. Yes but your mother won the genetic lottery he says. Cholesterol problems are very infrequently related to genetics says Frea. That's true says Moana. Well let's just wait and see what my doctor says next time says our man. Then it'll be back to steak and potatoes for me he says. And back to cholesterol problems says Moana. Why are you trying to deny me every little comfort he asks. Because I love you and want to grow old with you she says looking at him sternly. Regin looks over at his daughter. She nods her head at him. Can't argue with that he says. No you can't says Frea. They eat the remainder of their meal in silence.

They sit by the artificial fire in their living room. Regin has poured himself a whiskey. Frea and Moana are just keeping their father company. He watches the sports channel. Nothing much on but highlights. Regin likes football best. It's a man's sport. That's what he believes. Besides which he played it in high

66

school and college. Moana gets up. It is coming on quarter to the hour. That hour would be nine in the evening. Remember they left the house at half past nine in two straight lines. That's not true. You know that. But for Regin it becomes true. That's how our man remembers it. He knows they leave earlier at just after nine. They die at nine thirty. But for him they might as well have left at nine thirty.

Moana kisses him on the head. He looks up at her. I'm going upstairs to get ready for the play she says. He nods and smiles at her. Frea gets up. I think I'll get ready too she says. He looks at her and grins. What he says am I chopped liver. She smiles at him. I certainly hope not she says. She kisses him on forehead. Moana and Frea leave our man in his soft leather couch. His tumbler is almost empty. He takes the last sip and gets up. There is a commercial break. He goes over to the liquor cabinet and pours himself four fingers. Four fingers fills the tumbler. At least as full as you'd want to be seen as reasonable.

Our man comes back and sits down. He likes his whiskey. But you must remember that at this time he does not like it as much as he comes to. That's being kind. Regin comes to rely on alcohol to anesthetize himself. He comes to abuse it. But now he sits in front of the television. His belly is full. The fire is caressing him with warmth. And the whiskey is making him feel wobbly and sleepy. Shortly after his wife and daughter leave our man thinks he might go to bed. He is usually early to bed early to rise. He believes that this is part of his success. The early bird gets the worm his father always said. Regin lived that as best he could. It probably helped he was an early riser by nature. But one can't help but to think that the early bird might also get caught by the early cat. And what if the worm is not an early riser. But all of this speculation is moot. Our man is an early riser who believes it has contributed to his success. What he would give to have stayed up a few nights longer to spend time with his family.

Moana and Frea being night owls. These will be thoughts that haunt him for the months to come. Yet he cannot be blamed for being an early riser. He spent plenty of time with his wife and daughter. It's the outcome he's not happy with.

But now he sits on his leather couch. The skins of only the finest bovines. Carefully chosen skins that had no damage. But still murdered violently for their skins. One wonders if we'll come to view this as ghastly as we viewed the Nazis making lamp covers from the skins of dead prisoners. There is not much difference. In fact there is much in common. The callous disregard for life. The objectification of the being. The skin is merely the veil through which the soul should shine brightly. When that time has come and gone like a well worn suit it should be folded up and packed away. Into the ground to meld or into the fire to ash. But humanity's barbarism knows no bounds. You'll forgive me for being preachy. I now see things that might be dim for you. But from here things are obvious. The truth is blindingly bright.

There is death all around us. Continually things are being born and dying. Yet we feel eager to increase the violence and the demise. This is not our role. If anything our role is to protect and perhaps stanch the flow of loss. But as Regin sits casually on the hides of several bovine. He like most of us remain blind to the bloody hand that still grips the sharp knife. That steak that he craves was once the muscle of a sentient ruminant. He is blind to that too. He is blind and deaf to the squeals and the stench of the slaughterhouse. Yet tug at the corner of this fabric of life and everything unravels. For everything is connected. These are the butterfly wings I speak of. The soft beating causing tsunamis.

We walk like zombies amongst the living reality of this interconnectedness. This is our man's error. Indeed it is all our errors. Not to say that if our man had lived with more empathy and more consideration towards life that his wife and daughter would not have died tonight. That cannot be determined. But I wouldn't be telling this story if he had. For if his heart was more expansive. If his soul saw itself in the mirror of other living beings our man would not have taken his own life. This I am assured of. This I can assure you of. If you've travelled this far with me you know I can be a little preachy. But you'll forgive me realizing the height of these stakes. This is a matter of life and death. And though we stand at the stream of life like helpless children unable to swim. We should be adamant not to gut her life at its banks. For the blood of violence stains the soul. And this stain cannot be washed by prayers and supplications. No. The stain can only be washed by the current of the ages. The turbulent current that carries us through the doors of time.

Let us rejoin our man as he sits and sips on whiskey. His belly is warm and his head a little fuzzy. He picks up the remote and idly starts channel surfing. This is our man Regin unaware that these last few minutes will be the most precious of his life. And how casually he lets them slip through his fingers like a child playing on an infinite expanse of sand. But he does not know. And he cannot be faulted for this.

Moana and Frea come back down the stairs. It is nine oh one. He has just these two last minutes with them and he does not know it. And if he did would he prevent them from going. And if he prevented them from going would that save their lives. No gentle reader. We do not have the power to stave off death. And so it is good that we can only know the present and not the future. It is good that we have no foresight. Moana comes and stands in front of him. He looks up at her. She is ravishing in her blue dress. Her hair is done up in a bun and she wears simple jewelry. One does not wish to wear expensive jewelry on a night like tonight. Especially when one is riding the subway. And even though Regin will rue this day for taking their lives. He will wish with every ounce of his being that he had more forcefully urged them to take a cab there is nothing that can be undone. The subway is safe. And especially on this relatively short leg of the route there is no riffraff to contend with. On any other day he would not have given it a thought. He has ridden on the subway at all hours and days. It is amongst the safest in the world. And this part of it even safer.

You look wonderful he says. I wish I was accompanying you tonight he says. He stands up. We offered for you to come says Frea. He looks at his daughter. What a beautiful woman you have become he says. He kisses her on the forehead. I'll walk you to the door he says. I thought I would be busy tonight he says. Next time the three of us will attend together. Though the truth is he is not one who enjoys plays. But tomorrow he will wish that he went with them. He will wish that death had taken him too. Yet none of us know when death will come calling. Unless perhaps guided by our own hand. And that's what our man does doesn't he. We've seen that part already. This is a story that ends well. But travel with me gentle reader for this story starts off well. And it is the starting where we will end. I like to think of it as a new beginning. Too late for Regin Sigurd but not for the rest of us. Moana and Frea put on long black winter coats. They take a peek at themselves in the mirror as women do. Just to be sure that everything is in its place. Regin kisses his wife on the lips. Frea hugs him and kisses him on the cheeks. Goodbye Daddy she says. Goodbye he says. Have fun he says. He watches them leave. This is the last image he'll have of them. And it is of them walking down the hallway to the elevator. They turn one last time and he waves at them as they wave back. Then they're swallowed up by the elevator. And destiny leads them now.

Regin goes back into the living room. He still has two fingers of whiskey. He sits back down on the couch. He is bored with television. There is never anything good on he thinks. He turns it off and puts on the radio. Internet radio. He takes this all for granted like we all do. But these miracles of technology how quickly we become accustomed to them. How quickly they become pedestrian. And yet the world is full of wonder and awe. Our ability to rule our environment is a marvel. Yet we take it for granted. We grumble at the slowness of connections. Of signals bouncing from earth to space and back again. The few seconds. Such an annoyance. Like a child with too many presents at Christmas. We open them quickly. Each one new for a split second before the next. And within an hour all of them found lacking. All of them once again too familiar. But Regin is not grumbling. No. He is just trying to choose amongst the hundreds of choices. Finally he finds one. Not exactly what he wants. But the choices are too many and this station is close enough. It is easy listening jazz.

And he settles in to listen. On several occasions he wonders where Moana and Frea might be on their trip. We'll get to them soon enough. But first let us spend some time with our man Regin. Oblivious as his world is about to shatter around him. Cocooned up in his warm majestic home. With a belly full of healthy food. A glass of whiskey in his hand and pleasant music tickling his ears. He plans to wait up until they get back. The play being about two hours give or take. They should be home just before one. That is a stretch for him. He would likely not be awake by that time. But that is of no concern. For tonight he will be awoken from his couch at a little after ten. He doesn't remember the exact time. It was ten ten. That's when the police notified him of the incident.

But we get ahead of ourselves. Regin is enjoying some time to himself. And he does enjoy it. But only in small amounts. He is more of an extrovert. He likes being around people. Especially he enjoys his family. We have seen that already. Regin's eyes feel heavy. He is usually in bed by ten and at the moment it is nine fifteen. On most nights he might be reading the newspaper. But tonight is a Sunday. A day of rest. And he likes to take it easy. He is not a religious man though he is affiliated with a church. You'll only see him there twice a year. Perhaps more often if he's feeling needy. Easter and Christmas you can count on. And he comes with a big check. And he is well liked for his largess and his success. This despite Matthew chapter nineteen verses twenty-three through twenty-six. You know the one. It is easier for a camel to go through the eye of a needle than for a rich man to enter the Kingdom of God. And yet everywhere the rich are praised. For their work ethic and for their successes. Even in the sacred temples. How easily we offer alternative meanings to parts of scripture we dislike.

But I tell you solemnly. It is easier for a camel to thread itself through a needle than for a rich man to pass through the final door. I tell you truly that focusing on material gain and monetary success blunts spiritual growth. And it is this growth that gives you the keys to the final door. But few of you will listen. Less of you will agree. And this is your error. This is also our man Regin's error. Not to say that hard work is not important. It is. Not to say that you should avoid riches. But that should never be the focus. For many it is the focus. And that is the path to hell. Not paved with good intentions. Paved with the fake baubles of monetary focus. Yet again I digress. You cannot solely blame Regin's problems on his focus on wealth. Though it is clear that it has clouded his judgment. Right from the beginning. We'll see how it taints him. Starts as a small stain that spreads like a virus. Making one poor decision. The first link in that neverending chain. Yet all along the way opportunities to sever the links. And he does not. This is where he fails himself. We've seen that. The final failure. His giving up and tossing down the white flag. The flag of defeat. At his own hand. Such sorrowful waste. But you will not make such catastrophic decisions will you. Not if you bear with me. I am certain of it. Despite advice to the contrary we will learn from other's misfortunes and mistakes.

Now let us leave Regin slowly slipping into a nap. He is comfortable and relaxed. He is enjoying the last minutes of his ignorant bliss. We pick up this story gentle reader with Frea and Moana. They are waiting at the platform for the train. There are many people waiting with them. A few others are also heading to Broadway. Most are not. Most are just heading uptown to other bars and restaurants for late night entertainment. Many of you know that New York is eclectic. It is a Mulligan stew of different races and cultures. Of different languages and colors. This is New York's largess if one can use that term. It is what makes the city as successful and vibrant as it is. These are the tired and poor. These are the huddled masses yearning to breathe free. Many of you will recognize these words of Emma Lazarus from the Statue of Liberty. How nice. How wonderful these words roll off the tongue. How warm they make you feel. I do not jest. This is sincere. But on a night like tonight when such a calamity befalls the Sigurds it is difficult to remain inspired. Yet we must. We will.

The train pulls into the subway station. You notice that I do not identify the station. These are irrelevant details. They will distract you. You will try to seek meaning where no meaning is to be found. Do not worry about the minutiae. They will bog you down. It is the bigger picture we are interested in. Our man started down this road some time ago. Many years ago. And even though these things have been set into motion they cannot be changed. Not now. The dice have been cast. We can only watch. There may have been many forks upon this decision tree. But the last fork has just passed us by. As Frea and Moana step onto the train their fates have been sealed. All we do now is watch. We watch and wait. We carry on with this tale of tribulation and strife. Of woe and sorrow. We look for the small opportunities where the outcome might have changed. This is how we move forward upon our journey with greater clarity and less calamity. For a Sunday evening the train is quite busy. There is seating for everyone and even some seats gape empty. The mood is friendly and cordial. There are families and singles. There are the old and the young all riding the rails together.

I remember reading this play in high school says Moana. But I don't remember much of it she says. I do remember it being a tragedy though she adds. Frea looks at her mother and nods. Willy Loman is quite the tragic figure she says. But he brought most of it upon himself she says. Never a truer word has been said. He brought most of this upon himself. Even from the mouths of babes come words of wisdom. Though Frea is a woman I use the term liberally. He brought most of this upon himself. I do not mean to be unkind when I say that our man Regin has brought most of this upon himself.

You might wish to argue with me about Frea and Moana. You might like to suggest that they are mere pawns used in this tragedy to punish Regin. You wouldn't be far wrong. These are things I do not understand. Though Frea and Moana are not saints they are not sinners. And you are right to be concerned with how casually the fickle fingers of fate can toss them aside. All I can offer is that they suffered very little. Their journeys continue on with greater ease than our man Regin's. These are difficult philosophical questions to wrestle but I think in time you might come to understand. Moana and Frea were never the victims here. Even though they might seem victimized. Perhaps I use hyperbole. There aren't really any victims in our story. Regin is not victimized either. Rather his life is the outcome of his choices. I have said this before. He has made many errors. He continues to make errors. We have already seen the final error he made. That's how we started this tale. But you will not. You will not make these errors because you will learn from Regin's mistakes.

Is it not curious how Frea can make such a wise comment without knowing it. I think it is. She loves her father. She has never thought anything but the best of him. She does not think of him when she says that he bought it upon himself. She speaks only of the play. Only of Willy Loman. Yet are there not thousands perhaps millions of Willy Lomans out there. Yes there are. That was a rhetorical question. Regin Sigurd is very much a clone of Willy Loman. He has brought this upon himself. He has brought much goodness to his life. I do not mean to suggest that he is a man incapable of decent choices. I do not mean to suggest he is a man that can only make errors. There is no tragedy in that. To be sure there are man and woman who flit from one bad decision to another. Like a fly flitting from one Venus flytrap to the next. But these types are not tragic figures. No. They are comical. But Regin and his ilk are tragic. They are tragic because they have the ability to change. They just don't. That is the tragedy. The chrysalis promised potential that never blossoms. That is the tragedy.

The train travels upon the tracks. The gentle swaying motion is comforting. It is familiar. Perhaps it reminds us of our early travels in our mothers' wombs. This is just a guess. The clickety-clack of the track and the ebb and flow of the journey. The slowing down and now stopping at the station. The hemorrhaging of passengers. The influx of others. The train maintains an equilibrium of riders. There are twenty-one in this car. Including Moana and Frea.

I wonder if we should have seen the matinee says Frea. The play is quite long and there's school tomorrow she says. Moana looks at her and smiles. You were the one who wanted to attend this evening she says. Frea looks down at her fingers in her lap. I know she says. It sounded like a good idea at the time she says. It is a good idea says Moana. When is your class tomorrow asks Moana. Nine thirty says Frea. So you're just be a bit tired tomorrow and you can get to bed early tomorrow night says Moana. You are young and resilient says Moana.

Though she is not resilient enough to overcome the grim reaper. Oh what they would give for just another day to feel tired. Such a small thing. So inconsequential to feel tired for a day. So much easier than being dead. The train slows down again. Moana looks at Frea. Just one more stop she says. Frea looks up as they enter the station. She smiles. That didn't seem to take long she says. I know says Moana. Frea looks at her watch. It is almost nine thirty. This is the last time she'll look at her watch. The actual time is nine twenty-eight and thirty-seven seconds. Blessed are the ignorant for it is sometimes a real blessing. In less than two minutes Frea and Moana and eleven others on this car will be dead. None of them know it. That is a lie. One of them knows it. Just before the doors close a man walks into the car. He looks around nervously. He is a young man. He is nineteen. The same age as Frea. A trickle of sweat snakes down the side of his cheek. He is Lebanese. But that seems like such a long time ago. This young man's names is Fadi. Fadi can mean savior or sacrificer. Fadi believes this is his destiny. Fadi Hajjar. He is five feet nine inches. He is a good looking young man. His complexion is the color of light roasted coffee beans. He likes coffee. It is one of his fondest memories. Sharing coffee with his mother and uncles. He never knew much of his father. That is a story that is yet to come.

Fadi Hajjar's upper lip is damp. It is not that he is trying to grow a mustache. It is rather that he has not shaved. His upper lip has dark soft downy hair. His lips are full and he licks them. They feel dry. His mouth feels dry. His underarms are wet. He is nervous. And he is right to feel nervous. For he is about to commit an atrocity. He has big brown eyes. His hair is the color of wet coal. It is curly. It is hair that both men and women envy. When you look at Fadi you see naïveté. Those big brown eyes. You can see them on the boy he once was. The young boy. The toddler even. You can see them looking up at his father. His father has just come home and Fadi is excited to see him. His father looks much like Fadi looks now on this train. The apple has not fallen far from the tree. Fadi's father was a successful man. We will get to him in time. He worked at an oil refinery in Lebanon. Not far outside of Beirut. It was a good job. He worked hard. It was manual labor but he enjoyed it. For what it was it paid well. All things considered. But not all things were considered. You'll understand that later.

Fadi fidgets nervously with the sleeve of his white down jacket. It is new. It is as white as the driven snow. In just a few moments it will be as white as the driven snow with the red of carnage. As if a wolf had just gutted a rabbit all over it. You see this image. The rabbit's blood dotted all over the white snow. Does it make you uncomfortable. Perhaps a little. As it should. But does it make you as uncomfortable as to what is to come. I doubt it. And that is a pity. For a severed human hand should be just as ghastly as a severed rabbit's paw. But that is humanity's error. We can be forgiven for sympathizing more with our own kind. That is understandable. But we cannot be forgiven for turning a blind eye to the slaughter of millions of innocents that wear feathers or fur instead of skin. That is our tragedy and shall be our comeuppance. But this is not about the slaughter of animals as much as I wish to impress upon you the similarity. No. This is about human atrocities. Just as horrific but no worse.

Fadi has bought new clothes today. He is wearing them. His red sneakers. Nary a scuff upon them. His white down jacket as I just mentioned. Pristine. White as a virgin's wedding dress. But do not be misled. Fadi does not dream about virgins dancing in his head. Though he is well aware the virgins await him in the afterlife. But that is not why he has chosen this path. His father would not condone such a path were he alive. No. Fadi is the man who has grown from the poisoned roots of his childhood. We will get to that in good time. One cannot look at this man and say he is evil. For even though he is about to commit an atrocity he is not in his soul an evil man. We like to see monsters. It is only monsters that commit atrocities. They are monsters we declare. We are more enlightened. The they of course can be anyone. In this case it is Fadi the Muslim man. And this will be important. His Islamism. But really that is just a small part of why he commits this atrocity.

Fadi looks around and moves towards the farthest side of the car. Why does he do this. He does this because that is where most of the people are. He sees Frea and Moana. Frea looks up at him and smiles. He quickly averts his gaze. Frea smiles because he seems scared. There is something about him that Frea finds vulnerable. And he is vulnerable. He has been vulnerable to poor decisions since he was four years old. That is to come. But he cannot look at her. To do that would acknowledge her humanity. He cannot allow that. It would melt his resolve. It is truly difficult to look someone in the eye and kill them. There are names for people like that. Psychopaths. They are the closest that we come to being monsters. But Fadi is not a psychopath. He is not inherently a bad man. He is misinformed. He is confused and he is full of anger hate and vitriol. Do not misunderstand me. I do not make excuses for him. I state the facts. If I am dispassionate it is because we need to understand the facts. Emotions will color the experience. It will prejudice against what can be learned.

Underneath his jacket Fadi is hot. Most of the passengers have unbuttoned or unzipped their jackets. Fadi's is zipped up right to his neck. Frea looks at him again and furrows her brow. Then she looks over at her mother. Moana also has a quizzical look on her face. Fadi does not look at them. He is fiddling with the hem of his white jacket. The tubes of down run horizontally around his torso. If you look carefully. And Frea is looking carefully. There is something about the jacket. It is too big for him. It is brand new. And yet it is too big. Frea cannot understand why. If it were a used jacket you could understand. You could say that this man is poor and so he has no other choice but to accept hand me downs. But this jacket is new. All of Fadi's clothes are new. They are not high end but they are new. So this confuses Frea. She looks back at him. Fadi is looking down at the ground. He needs to act quickly. That is what he thinks. But then he thinks he will wait until the next station. There will likely be more people on the platform. He is right about this. He licks his lip. Frea sees another bead of sweat slip down his sideburn and cheek. She is now both a little confused and a little worried. She tries to dismiss her worry. Fadi is not big. He does not look menacing. He is not staring angrily at anyone. He is moving his lips. But Frea cannot hear what he is saying.

Fadi is saying prayers. Frea now thinks that perhaps he is mentally unstable. This calms her down. It explains his odd appearance. His odd social etiquette. But it calms her fears. This is her error. Though nothing might be done. She should listen to that tiny voice inside her. That one that raised concern. It was spot on. Fadi holds onto a pole in the middle of the car. Absentmindedly he kicks his foot at it. It doesn't make a sound. At least not that can be heard above the clacking of the train on its tracks.

Fadi is deep in thought. He is back in Lebanon. He is a small boy. Around four years old. He and his mother and his father are enjoying a picnic in the park. It is a warm sunny day. He is lying down. They have finished eating. His father is sitting beside him. His father is talking to his mother. But he cannot remember what it was about. But they are happy. He can tell this. They are smiling at each other. He knows that his mother and father love each other. He knows that they love him. He looks over at his father. The sun is right behind his father's head. His father turns to look at him. The sun creates a halo behind his father's head. His father is smiling at him. He can faintly see his father's bushy mustache and brown eyes looking at him. But the rest of his father's face is in shadows. This is because the sun is saturating his retinas with light. Fadi at four years old does not know this. I am adding this to create context. Would you like to kick the soccer ball Fadi's father asks him in Arabic. Fadi knows that his father spoke English and French. Fadi's French is not very good. Enough to get by in a pinch. His English is excellent. But he thinks in Arabic.

Four-year-old Fadi nods and says yes Daddy. His father holds out his hand and Fadi places his small hand in his father's. His father helps him up and picks up the soccer ball. As they walk past his mother his father kisses his mother on the top of her head. I think you are a good soccer player says Fadi's father. Fadi looks up at him and grins. Go chase it down his father says as he kicks it away from them. Fadi lets got of his father's hand and sprints for the ball. Fadi's father looks on with the pride that only fathers can feel. Fadi is fast for his young age. He stops the ball and spins around. He is many feet away from his father. He kicks the ball back to him. His father grins and nods. His father runs up to the ball and stops it. You will play with The Cedars one day I am sure Fadi's father says to him. This is the generosity of loving fathers. But there is also some truth in it. Fadi would have been good enough to play for the National Football team. But things don't work out that way.

Fadi's father kicks the ball back to him. Fadi is quick to it and he kicks it back. There are only a few things in his young life that Fadi loves. He loves his father and his mother. He loves his country and he loves Allah. And after that he loves football the most. But by the time he is five Fadi never plays football again. We will come to understand why in good time.

Fadi is awoken out of his reverie. He realizes that a tear has run loose from his eye. He wipes it self consciously. Frea has noticed and she looks away. Not that she is not comfortable with others' pain. She is. But she wishes to give him some privacy. The train is coming to a stop. That is what has brought Fadi out of his reverie. He slips his fingers inside the right arm of his jacket. He can feel the ignition button dangling like a cold serpent. He grabs it and pulls on the slack. His hand comes out from inside his jacket and he is holding the cylindrical switch. The red button on the end is apropos. Soon much of that which is around him will be colored red.

With his left hand Fadi reaches into his jean pocket. He pulls out a photograph. It is wallet-sized. It is well worn. The corners are frayed. Creases of time like veins angle across it. Fadi looks at the photograph. It is black and white. It is a photograph of his father. The only one he has. He rubs his thumb over the image. The cylindrical switch is now warm in his hand. It feels tacky. He now feels hot under all these clothes. He looks up. Many are gathering not far from where Fadi is. They are close to the door. They wish to disembark. This is his opportunity. Fadi is worried now. He has a lump in his throat. He has second thoughts. He is not certain that he can go through with this atrocity. Yet he has practiced this situation thousands of times in his mind. He practiced dressing for this occasion many times. It took him weeks to build his bomb corset. He can feel it tight against his torso and abdomen. He knows this is the end of the line for him. There are no more trains to catch once he detonates the bomb. He looks at his father. He is worried now. Fadi frowns. Frea watches him. He seems odd. She is not sure what is wrong with him. Frea watches Fadi's lips start to move.

La il laha il Allah Muhammad a rasool Allah Fadi says softly.
Frea frowns looking at him. There is no God but Allah Fadi says
and Muhammad is his messenger. Fadi is louder now but he is
not shouting. A couple of the passengers look up at Fadi. Frea is
beginning to get nervous. Fadi reaches up with his left hand
which still clutches the photograph of his father. He reaches up
for his zipper. La il laha il Allah Muhammad a rasool Allah Fadi
says again. He has found his confidence. He is speaking very
loudly now. Everyone in the car can hear him. Fadi pulls down
the zipper. His white jacket opens up. Frea gasps involuntarily.
She sees the explosives. She sees the wires. She knows what this
is without ever having seen it before. La il laha il Allah
Muhammad a rasool Allah Fadi says again. Moana screams. She
grabs Frea. But you must understand that all of this takes less
than a few seconds. Frea and Moana are trying to exit their seats.
The train is slowing down. It is in the station now. The
passengers on the platform are waiting to board. Some of them
step up. This is their error. This will not help them. A young man
in gray coveralls looks up. Ariel is embroidered over his left
chest in red cursive thread. This is Ariel Erez. He is recently from
Israel. Interestingly his last name means cedar. Like The Cedars
of which we heard earlier. This is just coincidence. But Ariel's
bravery is not coincidence. He has seen too much of this in his
homeland. Ariel has come for a new life in America. He is
heading to work. He is a janitor on the graveyard shift. Not any
more. What an odd euphemism. Graveyard. Ariel is going to his
shift from ten until six in the morning. He is literally going to his
grave. Going to the graveyard but he only understood it as a
euphemism. How this euphemism has become reality.

Fadi puts his hands up as if he is under arrest. As if he is
giving up. And in a way he is. In his mind he is giving himself up
to his fate. Frea can now see the red button just below Fadi's
right thumb. She closes her eyes shut tight. Moana is grabbing at

her forearm. She is trying to pull herself and her daughter off the train. Bismika Allahumma amutu wa ahyaa says Fadi. Fadi closes his eyes. Ariel has launched himself from his seat. He is not far from Fadi. You can see him reaching for Fadi. But he is still too far. His effort is valiant. But he will not succeed. His goal was to tackle Fadi to the ground and use his own body as a shield. Ariel is brave. But he is not quick enough and he is too far away. Allahu Akbar says Fadi. He sees his father in his mind's eye. Allahu Akbar he says again. His thumb presses down on the red button. That is the last thing he does.

Died twelve little people in two straight lines. Right on that train at half past nine. There are really thirteen dead. If you count Fadi. But Fadi was not innocent he knew what was to come. It's the twelve other people now dead and numb. That's all there is. There isn't anymore.

I do not wish to focus on the macabre. The scene is awful. There are many wounded. They cry out in pain and agony. It is smoky and the stench is nauseating. Some try to find an exit. They trip over severed limbs and slip on wet blood. I'll not say anymore. This is a ghastly sight. Many of the survivors will suffer post traumatic stress. As any sane person would who has had to deal with such violence. Such macabre images. But let us not dwell on this suffering. If one can be grateful for small mercies. And I'll leave that up to you. Then one can be grateful that Moana and Frea are at least not suffering. We are an interesting lot. Humanity that is. We try to make sense of the senseless. The survivors will try to make sense of this event. Our man Regin tries the same but he is ineffective. Look at numbers for an example. We start sifting through numbers looking for patterns. Looking to make sense of things. And numbers offer that. If even only through coincidence. For example. It was nine oh three when Moana and Frea left the house. It had just gone nine thirty when Fadi pressed his thumb to that red button. This is how

Regin tries to make sense of things. For months our man Regin uses the lines from a children's book as a prayer. He repeats them as if he were saying a rosary. Though he is not Catholic. You have heard this before. In an old house in Manhattan that was covered with vines he says. Lived two little girls in two straight lines he says. They left the house at half past nine he says. That's all there is he says. There isn't anymore he says.

Those lines come from Frea's favorite series of books about Madeline. Of course our man Regin has bastardized them and changed them somewhat. But they spill from his lips like wine from the chalice. They spill from his lips with every breath. Regin says them so often he has become obsessive and compulsive about it. Until he does not say them anymore. In a very real sense those words anchor him to reality. They are literally the breath that gives him strength to carry on. But only for a little over two months. One cannot live in denial forever. And our man Regin does not know how to forgive. He does not know how to move forward. He also does not know the power of butterfly wings. But we'll get to that in good time.

For now we must revisit Regin as he lies relaxing at home on the couch. His tumbler of whiskey is empty. It lies on the coffee table off to the side of the couch that our man is lying on. Regin has nodded off. He allowed himself to as he wanted to be awoken when his wife and daughter come home. Regin is dressed in a light blue shirt. It is plain blue. He prefers not to wear too much flashy clothes. However he makes exception with his socks. Tonight his stocking feet are covered in blood red socks. He will never where red again after tonight. The red does not clash with his navy pants. But they do stick out. That is his one splash of color. He always wears brightly colored socks that sometimes clash with the rest of his outfit. Though you cannot often see his socks unless he is sitting down. Regin's hands are folded over his belly. One is on top of the other. You might say he looks like he

RED REIGN

would if he were in a casket. He is still as death. Only the slow rising of his belly gives away his tenuous grip to life.

There is a loud and some would argue obnoxious knocking on the door. Bang bang bang. Three knocks. It startles Regin. He wakes and rubs his eyes not sure what has woken him. Bang bang bang. Regin looks over at the door. Just a minute he shouts. God dammit he says under his breath who could it be. He was having a warm and joyful nap. He does not remember the dream but he is filled with what feels like warm honey. Our man Regin looks at his watch. It is ten ten. The analog hands point a sharp V. Who could it be he thinks. He walks up to the front door and peers through the peephole. He sees the stretched out shape of a police officer. One of New York's finest. The officer is dressed more sharply than Regin has seen them dressed on the street.

Regin unlocks the door and opens is up. The officer is the same height as Regin. He is also about Regin's age. That is not entirely correct. The officer is forty-nine. His birthday is coming up on September the ninth. He will then be fifty. This officer also looks good for his age. He keeps himself fit and rested for his demanding job. This part here is the worse part of his job. He has done many of these. And he has enjoyed none of them. But it is his responsibility to inform next of kin. Rather him with his years of experience and seniority than these new rookies still wet behind the ears. Regin smiles at the police officer but it is not a smile brimming with warmth. Our man looks at the officer's uniform. Just under his shield is a nameplate. It says Dullahan in all capitals.

Officer Dullahan takes off his cap. May I come in please he asks Regin. Regin nods and gestures for him to enter with his right hand. Yes of course sorry says Regin. Dullahan steps into the entrance way holding his cap in both hands in front of him. I'm Captain Michael Dullahan he says. Dullahan does not offer his hand in greeting. Regin tenderly puts his out. Dullahan finds this

85

awkward. He takes Regin's hand and shakes it quickly. May we sit down asks Dullahan. Regin nods. Of course he says. May I get you a drink asks Regin. I mean a soft drink or a glass of water. Dullahan shakes his head slowly and wearily. No thank you he says. Regin gestures again with his right hand and leads Dullahan to the dining room table. It was just over an hour ago that he sat at this table. Not with a police officer but with this wife and daughter. Soon Regin will sell everything. He will move to a hotel to live. The only thing he will keep will be a Madeline doll. An old one that was once Frea's.

Regin sits down. Dullahan sits down. Regin rests his forearm on the table and holds his hands together. He notices a small piece of beef. It is not real beef. It is the fake beef from the Shepherd's pie earlier. Regin takes a napkin from the napkin holder and wipes up this small morsel. He folds the napkin into an abstract origami shape and puts it to his left. It almost looks like a crane. Regin has nine hundred and ninety-nine to make if he wants his wish to come true. And he wants his wish to come true. He does not know yet. But his wish will be to turn back time. Change the outcome. But as we know. If wishes were horses then beggars would ride. Regin looks up at Dullahan. Are you sure I can't get you something to drink he asks. Dullahan shakes his head. I am sure he says. Regin is getting nervous now. One never likes a visit from the police. But there is something dour about Dullahan's manner. Dullahan places his cap on the table to his right. It does not look like origami.

Dullahan looks over at Regin. He does not smile. His face is the stone mask of a man carrying a heavy weight. You are Regin Sigurd he asks. Regin looks at him and frowns just a small frown. Our man nods his head just a little. I am he says. What is this about he says. Your wife is Moana Sigurd and your daughter is Frea Sigurd asks Dullahan. He looks softly but intensely at Regin. Regin nods his head again. Yes he says. What is this about he says. Dullahan swallows and his Adam's apple bobs up and down like a float tugged at by a fish. There was an incident on the train this evening says Dullahan. What kind of incident asks Regin. Regin's arms are like blocks of glass attached to the table. He looks at Dullahan. What sort of incident he asks again. Our man Regin does not recognize his own voice. It seems foreign to him. It is a child's voice. The voice of a scared child. But why is he scared.

We believe there was a terrorist attack on the subway tonight says Dullahan. Regin looks at him unblinking. There have been thirteen confirmed dead. We believe that Frea and Moana are amongst the dead. I'm sorry says Dullahan. I am very sorry. Regin stares at him unblinkingly. Our man does not say anything for a while. Miles of openness stretch out between him and Dullahan. It feels like he is looking at Dullahan from very far away. Did he hear him properly. I beg your pardon says Regin. What do you mean he asks. I know this must come as a shock says Dullahan. Regin interjects. You must be mistaken he says. My wife and daughter are at a play in Broadway he says. They're watching Death of a Salesman as we speak he says. Dullahan's eyes look wet. Like wet gray stones set in his head. This is often how it goes. The denial. The confusion. Then comes the anger and the pain.

A suicide bomber blew himself up on the train this evening says Dullahan. We believe your wife and daughter were on that train. Dullahan will become more pointed. He will become blunter. Oftentimes that is the only way to get through to the next of kin. You're gravely mistaken says Regin. Like I said my wife and daughter are watching a play. Dullahan and our man Regin watch each other. Not with anger or prejudice. No. Each stares at the other solid in their belief that the truth will persuade the other of their mistake. Regin is mistaken. He does not have truth on his side. When it has come to truth he has walked next to him with a crooked stride. Regin is not intimate with truth. Not like Dullahan. Though Dullahan has kept his distance from truth he has walked miles with him. He has looked at him through clear eyes. Seen truth's smiles and his many trials.

We are confirming the identities of the victims of this terrorist attack says Dullahan. It will take some time. I would like to ask you if we might obtain some DNA from both your wife and daughter says Dullahan. A hair from their head or even their toothbrushes. So you don't know says Regin. You don't know it is them. Dullahan continues to look at our man Regin through wet steady eyes. Eyes that have seen the depths of depravity of the human soul. Eyes that he wishes were sometimes blind. We found their identifications in the wreckage says Dullahan. His voice is hollow but calm and steady. Regin feels he is listening to him from far away. Down some dark tunnel. We found their drivers' licenses says Dullahan. That must be a mistake says Regin. Yet slowly all around him his world is slowly crashing down. He breaks his stare with Dullahan. And with it breaks his fragile hold on denial. His eyes brim with tears but he stifles them. He blinks several times quickly. The back of his nose gets hot and tingly. Someone clamps his windpipe with a hot steel band. He coughs trying to dislodge the pain. He looks back at Dullahan.

Are you sure asks Regin. Dullahan nods his head. I am certain he says. How can you be certain asks Regin. We have video footage of your wife and daughter entering the car that the suicide bomber entered says Dullahan. We have their identifications. It is now just a matter of confirming their identity says Dullahan. For that we need DNA he says. Regin looks at Dullahan. His eyes as wet as river stones. Can I see them he asks. It is a plea. Dullahan hates this part. He does not know how to respond. I do not recommend that he says. It might not be possible he adds. That is up to the Medical Examiner he says. Why can't I see them Regin asks again. Do not go down this path thinks Dullahan. He knows what bombs do to fragile soft flesh at close proximity. Your wife and daughter would be hard to recognize says Dullahan. I would still be able to recognize them says Regin. They are not as you remember them says Dullahan. He does not know how to discuss this with Regin. They are my wife and child says Regin his voice getting as hot as he can muster. Dullahan does not engage. As I said says Dullahan that will be up to the Medical Examiner. In the meantime may I get some DNA from your wife and daughter he asks. A toothbrush or hairbrush he says. Even both would be better he adds.

Regin gets the items for Dullahan who puts them each in a separate envelope. I am very sorry he says again. Dullahan fishes for a couple of cards from his pocket. He hands the first one to Regin. Regin accepts it. This is my card says Dullahan. If you need anything please call me. Dullahan is gracious and generous that way. It does not matter though he has never been called after incidents like this. He hands the second card to Regin. This is the number for our crisis counselors he says. If you need them you can call them anytime day or night he says. Someone from that department will call you tomorrow says Dullahan. But if you need help before then please call he says. Dullahan looks at Regin. They are standing in the hallway. Regin is a shadow of himself. He is ghostly white. His mind is a mischief of mice in a complicated maze. Dullahan looks at him carefully. Dullahan has seen this many times before. He knows that Regin has hardly heard him at all. Do you understand what I've said Dullahan asks. Regin looks up at him vacantly. He looks at him as if it were the first time he has seen Dullahan. Regin nods his head. Yes Regin says.

What did I say asks Dullahan. Regin looks down at the cards in his hand. You said you will call tomorrow says Regin. No says

Dullahan. One of our crisis counselors will call says Dullahan. Will you be okay tonight asks Dullahan. Dullahan looks at Regin carefully. He is looking for some surety that Regin will be around tomorrow. Regin looks at him and nods. Dullahan has found his answer. I am very sorry for your loss says Dullahan. Dullahan puts on his cap and opens the door. He closes it softly behind him. Regin stares at the closed door for many minutes. He is numb. It is as if he is standing next to himself. He sees himself as a wax figure. He is empty. He still does not quite understand that his wife and daughter are dead. That reality will start to settle in over the next few days.

Regin turns around after a long time and goes back to the couch and sits down. He turns on the television and he stays like that until the sun comes up. Then he cries and he vomits and he cries until his eyes are red and dry as sandpaper and the well of his sorrow is empty of tears. And that is the beginning of the end for our man Regin. We know the rest. But this is a story that started at the end. And so we must continue on our journey towards the beginning. Let us turn then to better times.

More of the Middle

This is our man Regin during one of his happiest moments. At least one of his happiest moments related to work. Not long ago he was promoted to Vice President of International Business. Sometimes they call it International Development. That is a minor difference. Of no real consequence. That was shortly after his handling of the Beirut Dilemma as it became known. But that was a long time ago. That was fifteen years ago. But just three years ago we visit Regin during a happy moment. Remember we are working backwards. So we will get to the Beirut Dilemma. That is the crux of the matter really. You could say it is the lever upon which Regin's world destroyed itself. You will see that in good time. Fifteen years after the Beirut Dilemma Regin's wife and daughter lie dead in a mangled train car in a subway station in New York City. This is how life is intertwined. But you can't know that at the time. But I'll show you how. Never underestimate the power of small decisions to create big consequences.

But again I get ahead of myself. You will forgive me. But I must offer tapas of what is to come. If only to keep you by my side on this journey. So that is just a little morsel of what is to come. The Beirut Dilemma. The name explains it all really. As you will come to understand. So now let's take a moment to refresh our memories. You will remember when we started that our man Regin was being attended to by a medic. That man's name was Adelmo. You will recall that Adelmo was rescued of the waters of Florida by a man in a yacht. That man was Anzu Buer. That happened thirty years ago. Anzu Buer is the founder of Anzu Inc. Anzu started the company that bears his name over fifty years ago. It is a multibillion dollar oil refining business. There is good money to be made in oil. Anzu Buer knows this. He is on the Forbes list. In fact he makes it into the top fifty regularly. Regin knows this because he gets paid well. He makes a lot of money. But this calf of capitalism. This golden calf of capitalism if you will. This calf we worship. A false god and a false idol exacts more than its pound of flesh. It poisons our environment and it sacrifices men women and children. The Beirut Dilemma is a classic example of this. You will see what I mean in good time.

So Adelmo was rescued by Anzu and it is Anzu the man and corporation that one could say is indirectly responsible for our man's death. Though to be fair Regin must take the greatest share of ownership. He did after all did he not tie his shirt around his own neck and take his own life. That is not a rhetorical question. He did. He killed himself. He committed suicide. And the many errors in judgment he made. The very many have led him down this slippery path all paved in gold. So we will assign most of the blame to our man Regin. But we must also dust Anzu with some as you will come to see. Anzu Buer has been retired for some ten years. More or less. He plays an important role on the board. He is still Chairman. He persuades the rest of the board of Anzu Inc. over whom they should hire as CEO. Just before Anzu retired. This is about ten years ago. He handpicked Christian Camael. It was a divisive pick. Most of the board were against Camael as CEO. They called him too soft. He was too much of an environmentalist. He cared too deeply about his employees and not enough about the bottom line. Bottom line being what's most important he was finally parachuted off. Replacing him was everyone's favorite our man Regin. This happened three years ago.

Now when I speak of time past. You must understand I look back from the present. And the present is where this story started. In the police cell where Regin took his life. So ten years ago when Camael was elected CEO is only seven years from where this chapter takes place. This is the chapter where Regin becomes CEO and that was three years ago from present time. Present time always being Regin's suicide in the police cell where we started this tale of caution.

You will forgive me if I sometimes sound verbose. I don't mean to be. But I must be certain that we follow along together. That you're with me on this journey. I must be certain that everything is clear. Crystal clear. Or as clear as I can make it. Believe me it is difficult. It is difficult because language is like an Oldowan tool. It does the job but it is imprecise. It is blunt. And it is laborious. But this is all you have. And so I will do my best. Sometimes coincidences are kismet. Most times they are unimportant. Most times one could say that coincidences are nothing more than aboulic. Take for example the beginning of this story. The fact that Anzu Buer saves Adelmo who cannot save our man Regin. We might seek deeper meaning there. But there is none to be found. The only one who could have saved Regin is Regin himself. But it is interesting to note the coincidence. The merging and twining of paths. We like to look for meaning. We seek to make chaos dance before us to our own tune and our own bidding. But we cannot. Chaos dances to music we cannot hear nor understand. Like ants climbing an elephant's back we think the world is gray and flat. But that is the fault of our perspective. We do not have the foresight for greater understanding.

But this is all an aside. It is not necessarily our error that we seek to understand the unknowable. Because perhaps in time the unknowable will give us a glimpse of her naked self. We must strive. But we must also be diligent in our striving. We must be cautious that we do not take tiny mind and extrapolate it to omniscience. That would be a very grave error. Indeed. But I digress as I am wont to do. You will forgive me. But this story is powerful. There are abundant teaching opportunities within this tale of tribulation and titillation.

So we find ourselves three years from the present. We are in the same home where Regin and Frea and Moana were just before they left in two straight lines at half past nine for subway line. Of course everyone is younger now. Our man Regin is forty-nine. His wife Moana is forty-seven and their daughter Frea is sweet sixteen. It is early morning as we peek in on the Sigurds. It is six thirty-three in the morning. Regin is about to leave for work. He usually gets in by seven. Early to work late to leave and all that the company offers you will receive. You might say that is Regin's mantra. His motto. What he lives by. And it has proven valid thus far. He came up with it himself. Early on in his career. Frea is still sleeping. She will not awake for another half hour. Moana wakes with her husband as she has done since they were married. They have been married twenty-five years. But because we are three years behind on this morning they have been married only twenty-two years. But for these twenty-two years she has awoken at the same time as her husband. Not every day. There were days when they have not slept together in the same bed. Days when they have not even slept in the same house. Or same country. But we put the cart before the horse. We will get to that point. And this is not due to any infidelities. No. This is just the nature of Regin's work. His time spent on this vessel of the captains of industry. Though it is fair to say that Regin has two wives. Work and Moana. And sometimes Moana feels that she is the second wife. And this is not an incorrect feeling.

But let us return to the dining room table of the Sigurd home. Regin is eating turkey bacon and fake sausages. He is eating a slice of toast. The egg he longs for can no longer be found in the home. Already Moana is getting him onto a stricter diet. Already his cholesterol is too high. He thinks it is because of work stress. Moana believes it is because of his diet. She is right. But he doesn't grumble much anymore. She is a good wife. She takes care of her husband. And besides today he is meeting members of the board at the fanciest steak restaurant in town. He will make use of this golden opportunity. He knows what they might want to talk to him about. At least the rumor mill at work has been running rampant with the suggestion that he'll be promoted to CEO. Regin is cautiously optimistic. It is all he has ever wanted with Anzu Inc. Ever since he started with them. He cannot believe that it was twenty-five years ago he started as a Junior Account Executive right out of college. With a fresh face and a freshly minted commerce degree he stepped aboard the vessel that is Anzu Inc. At that time a much smaller company. At that time headed by the driven and relentless Anzu Buer. Twenty-five years from ordinary seaman to captain. It is a leap that few have managed. Our man Regin has managed it. He will now be a captain of industry. A peer amongst titans. That is how he views himself.

Regin finishes the last morsel of toast and the last morsel of sausage. He does not mind them. But they are a lacking facsimile of the real thing. He salivates as he thinks of the steak restaurant. Not only over the steak but also over the position. This breakfast will keep him partially full until lunch. He does not find a meal without real meat and eggs to be satisfying. But that like many things is his error. He holds his prejudices dear. He clings to them as though they were his little darlings. When in fact they are nothing more than demon spawn. This is true of all prejudices. The little darlings we care and love. The wolves in sheep's' clothing. The demons behind the vacant eyes and yawning smiles.

Regin looks over at his wife. That was a wonderful breakfast he says. Thank you he says. She smiles at him and gets up and clears away his plate. Regin remembers a time when she used to make him real breakfasts. Hearty breakfasts. When his plate was piled high with fried eggs. Two of them. Rashers of bacon. Enough so that he didn't need to count them. And not to be outdone he had sausages. Two big sausages. Not like the small fingers they give you now. It was a Noah's Ark of slaughtered animals. Almost one of each edible kind. Our man Regin does not notice that animals care as much for their own lives as he does for his. He does not notice that he is not destined to consume flesh. That a vegetable plant based diet will suffice. Nay. It will offer magnificent health. The diet of violence and blood. The diet of decaying flesh and effluence of animals' reproductive organs bites back. But he does not see that. Most of us don't. Nevertheless this is not an epistle about animal rights. Though such a moral tale would tell a similar story. No. This is a tale of tribulation. Though the tribulations and tremulations of murdered beasts are intertwined with the consternations and castrations of human lives.

Regin gets up from the table and replaces his chair. Before his daughter grew into a woman he would at this point visit her in her bed. He would kiss her on the forehead before he headed out the door. But that would be out of place now. It does not cross his mind. He doe not even think of it. He hasn't for some years now. Not since she was ten or eleven. Frea is different now. She is becoming a woman. And though she is still daddy's little girl she has changed. She has been pinched and stretched and rolled into something a little stiffer by the hands of time. This is youth. Old age gets rolled and pinched and patted into something softer by those same hands of time. This is the marching on of the years. This is how time sands and buffets out the coarseness of youth into the softness and roundness of age.

There is a buzz from the intercom. This is Regin's chauffeur. That is one of the perks of being a Vice President. Not for some time has Regin had to jostle with the riffraff in the subway on his way to work. Now he is picked up each morning in a black sedan. Regin likes to feel important. And he does feel important. Anzu Inc. makes him feel important and it gives him a large salary. This also makes him feel important. More important than he actually is. This is also one of his errors. But he is not arrogant. Let me not steer you astray. He means well and he is mostly kind but he feels somewhat superior. This cannot be helped. You pay a man an outrageous some for any job and he starts to feel that he deserves it. That this is his true value. It is not. His true value is in being human. In helping his fellow man. And when I say that understand that I mean fellow people. Both men and women. Our true value has always been in helping us move beyond the small and the petty. In moving towards the light. In helping each other move towards justice and equality and equanimity. But this whole system is absurd. The capitalist free market system is corrupt. And I do not say this as a communist. Do not misunderstand me. Capitalism is the best of the broken crutches we have at our disposal. But it is a crutch. We cannot truly release our destiny until we can let go of our crutches. Until we can all walk arm in arm in harmony and in equality. Where each is allowed to pursue their highest ideals. To contribute that song that is within their spirit safe in the knowledge that their needs are met. Until we can get to that place. Which is beyond capitalism and communism and any of the other isms. Until we can get beyond this infantile state of humanity we will continue to need to take heed of cautionary tales like this one of our man Regin.

But again I digress. Regin does not answer the buzzer. There is no need. His chauffeur will wait patiently in the black sedan until Regin is ready. Moana comes back from the kitchen. That was Yama she says. It is almost a question. Yes it is says Regin. Yama is his chauffeur. He has an unusual name. But perhaps it is not that unusual where he is from. He is from Northern India. His name is Yama Mara. He is a man in his early forties. He has two daughters. Their names are Tanha and Raga. Tanha is the oldest. She is twenty-one. Raga is nineteen. They are wicked women. They know nothing more than trying to seduce wealthy men. And they succeed more often than not. They have tried to seduce our man Regin. But if he is just one thing it is that he is faithful to Moana. They had no success. This was only two years ago at a company party. At Anzu Buer's large estate. We will not dwell on that. Nothing came of it. But they were lewd. Each of them seduced a member of the board. Not Anzu Buer but other members. Christian found them in a couple of the spare rooms. Each of them on their knees in front of a naked man. They were tasting carnal knowledge you might say. In the same room. It was not a good situation. It cost Anzu Inc. a pretty sum. As you can imagine. Raga was a minor at the time. Those board members were fired. Tanha and Raga made off with a tidy sum each. And yet. And yet Yama Mara remains employed. This is the strangeness of Anzu Inc. This is the ambivalence of capitalism to evil. This is considered the price of doing business. I do not mean to suggest that sex between two adults is evil. Do not misinterpret me. I only suggest that Tanha and Raga are evil. They worship at the altar of greed and money. They prey on married men. These two men with whom they indulged with fellatio were both married. Each had a child or two. They are not blameless. But you must understand. These are the sorts of errors one makes when one is not aware of the deeper meaning of this journey. This ride around the sun time and again. You might think I am being harsh. But I am not. I know of things that you do not know. I know that there is a battle being daily fought. Between the darkness and the light. Tanha and Raga fight valiantly for the dark. And we feeble humans. We too often succumb to darkness's might. We too easily give in. This is what happened with those two men. This is how Tanha and Raga find easy prey.

Moana comes and puts her hands on Regin's shoulders. She takes his tie in both her hands and adjusts it. It does not need adjusting. But it is a loving gesture. You have seen this before. She kisses him on the mouth. You won't be late tonight will you she asks. He looks at her and smiles. No I hope not he says. But I'll let you know he says. Good luck with your meeting she says. I know this is what you've wanted for a very long time she says. And you deserve it she says. Thank you my darling he says. He kisses her on the forehead. He walks to the door with her at his side. He puts on his jacket. He pauses one moment before he leaves. I love you he says. I love you too she says. He opens the door and the big wide world swallows him up. Moana goes back to the kitchen and finishes up her washing and cleaning. Frea will be up soon. Moana will get breakfast ready for her.

Outside this building our man Regin steps onto the sidewalk. The doorman nods his head at him. Regin does not notice. Not today. He has a lot on his mind. He is dreaming of gold coins and the best corner office. Yama Mara is standing by the car door. He grins widely at Regin. There is something about him that is creepy. But you cannot pinpoint it. So you brush it aside. He is not a tall man. Yama is five feet nine. He is thin. Perhaps even gaunt. If he were a woman you might even call him anorexic. He has long thin spindly fingers. The kind that might even be able to cut right into your flesh and pull out your heart. His black eyes are beady like a crows. They seem to stare right into your very soul and measure your worth. Yama opens the door for Regin. Good morning sir he says with sincerity. But underneath it all there is something sinister. You might think that Yama believes himself to be more elevated than you. And you'd be right. But you'd also dismiss the thought as both unkind and untrue. That would be your error. Yama closes the door on Regin his bony fingers letting the handle go. He turns to cross over and enter into the driver's door. His complexion is brown. It might remind you of ground coffee beans. Then you realize it more closely resembles brown coffee beans that have been stirred into an urn of cremains. There is an ashen gray undertone to his color. His hair is black and straight. It looks permanently wet. It is not. It is just very oily. And that sums up Yama. He seems oily and slippery. Like you just can't get a fix on him.

Yama starts up the car and turns into traffic. Has your morning been good so far sir he asks looking at Regin in the rearview mirror. Our man Regin is looking out the window. It's been fine thank you Yama he says. Good says Yama. That is very good sir he says again. There is something about Yama's voice that makes you wonder if he knows the details of the future. Nothing seems to surprise him. And indeed that is because nothing does. But on this glorious day. This glorious day for our man Regin he does not notice. Regin is not the most intuitive man. In fact his intuitions are blunted. Some would say stunted. That would be a fair comment. That would also be Regin's error. His blunted intuition or understanding of human nature has led him astray. More than once. The Beirut Dilemma comes to mind. Decisions he could have made differently. The course his life would have taken would have been different. But just as Regin sits in the back of the car thinking of sugarplums and fairies. So is he unaware of that Yama is a dark force. Like his daughters. One cannot say what Yama's goals are. He is hard to read. You might just think that he seeks to shoo away the light. To destabilize the good. You might say he enjoys misery. And as it has been said. Misery is lonely. It loves company. Yama relishes in the misery of others. He will come to delight in the death of Moana and Frea in that train car. He will come to delight in Regin's suicide. Not outwardly of course. But something in his shrunken black soul cannot delight in light. It feeds on the dark and the dank. But Yama would never be directly evil. He rather prefers to steer it in the right direction. For instance he wouldn't harm someone directly. But he would perform lesser evils if he thought he could get away with it. He skims a little extra as a chauffeur. He is paid salary but he is reimbursed for fuel mileage and maintenance. This is where he skims from the top.

Do not pity Yama. He is the captain of his own ship. He has freewill. And he has chosen darkness as his destiny. The point he fails to understand is that darkness will be his own destiny. Already he has cancer. It gnaws away silently but diligently in his bones. And it will start to nibble on his lungs in a year's time. That is when he will come to know of it. That is when his own darkness will come to take him home. And it will not be pleasant. It will take six years six months and six days for the cancer to kill him. And it will be painful and it will be hell. But do not delight in Yama's comeuppance. It has been wrought by his own hands. But life is not always just like that. Though this is a morality tale life is not moral. Life is not blind justice holding scales in her hands. Life is indifferent. And it is indifference that is perhaps most dark. And it is because of this we each need to be beacons of light. For though Regin is a good man. By most standards. He is punished just as harshly as Yama. Though perhaps more so. For he has lost two good souls. His wife and his daughter. Yama will leave both daughters and his wife behind. Perhaps you could say that is part of their punishment. But I fear I am getting preachy. Though this is a tale of trials and tribulations. It is not meant to

101

be a sermon. Though how many sermons have we ignored. And those too are our errors. But be foretold that life is not just. There is much injustice in it. You already know this. So let us bare the sword of justice and the shield of honor.

My daughters are hoping to get summer positions at Anzu says Yama. He knows it will happen. This is part of the settlement that he has with the company. For keeping quiet about his daughters. For remaining a loyal employee. Two years ago you will remember that his daughters were caught by the current CEO Christian Camael giving oral sex to two board members. So Yama has an ace up his sleeve. He is perhaps the second most powerful person employed by Anzu. One might say he is Anzu Buer's right hand man. That would be incorrect. But from this perspective it sometimes looks that way. Tanha hopes to work for you says Yama. He looks at Regin through the rearview mirror. His black beady eyes like darting wet marbles. Regin looks at him and smiles weakly. That is the last thing on his mind. I might not be in this position for much longer Regin says. I know says Yama Tanha hopes to be the CEO's assistant. She also hopes to compromise his morals. To take from Moana that which is dear to her. But Tanha will not succeed. Regin was born a handsome man. He had good hardworking parents and they taught him the value of hard work. Not to rest on your laurels. And his good looks were his laurels. He has been tempted many times and he has never once failed the test.

Regin frowns at Yama for a moment. He finds the certainty of his statement a little unnerving. I cannot take it for granted says our man Regin. Nothing has been announced yet he says. Yama smiles at him and shows white teeth. Teeth as white as the bleached bones of scavenged prey. Sharp as razor wire. These are only the rumors I hear says Yama. But I believe them he says. I have watched you work hard and diligently sir says Yama. There is no one more deserving he says. Regin looks out the window again. He notices that the road is wet. It was raining last night. The sky is still gray. The color of dour moods. Regin smiles small. I will certainly interview her for any summer positions that come up he says to Yama. You are a very kind man Mr. Sigurd sir says Yama. Regin does not say anything. Yama's voice sounds sincere to our man. But it is dripping with insincerity. He ingratiates himself like a viper slipping into your warm bed only to bite you at the first chance. But Regin is not aware of that. He does not have the sensitivity of an artist to intuit the insincerity of Yama. He sits in silence the rest of the way to the office. He does not appreciate Yama as his chauffeur. And rightly so. Yama is forward and too at ease. Regin would prefer it if he were a little more polished. A little more polite and distant as an employee should be. But Regin is not about to reprimand Yama. He does not think that would be appropriate. And he thinks that perhaps he is being too harsh. This is how we dismiss the small voice in our hearts that allows us to see things hidden from the eyes.

At the office in Manhattan Yama parks the car outside the front doors. It is an impressive building. It is in an impressive part of the world and New York City. It is a landmark you might say. Regin waits as Yama exits his door and comes round to the rear passenger side. He opens the door for Regin. Regin steps out. The usual time sir asks Yama. Regin pauses and looks at him for a moment. Probably not he says. I might be working a little late he says. I'll catch a cab our man says. I would be deeply upset sir says Yama with the same feigned indignation. I will wait for your call says Yama. I will be happy to pick you up at any time tonight sir he says. I am certain that there will be a celebration in your honor Yama says. Regin turns to enter the building. I will call you then he says. Thank you sir says Yama. And with that Regin disappears into the Anzu Inc. building in Manhattan. The thirty-third floor is where his office is.

He exits the elevator right into the main reception area. He nods and smiles at the receptionist. He does not remember her name so he does not stop to talk. He walks down the hallway to one of the side offices. He will soon be moving upstairs. That is our man Regin's hope. The thirty-sixth floor is where the C executives are. Regin walks into his office and closes the door. He looks around. There is not much to pack up. Regin is an efficient employee. He keeps a neat and tidy office. Spic and span. His mother and father always expected as much from him at home. It has served him well. The CEO's office is four or five times as large. Regin can't imagine what he'll do with so much space. Then he gently chastises himself. It is not a certainty he thinks. I should remain humble he thinks until it is made public. Even then he thinks. Even then I should remain humble he thinks. Nobody likes a braggart he thinks to himself. He hangs up his jacket and takes a seat behind his desk. The view out of his office is not bad. All the offices along the edge of the building have reasonable views. It is the Manhattan skyline after all. Regin looks at the picture of his wife and himself on the left of his desk. It was from a recent holiday they took. He remembers the time. It was a cruise. And this was a formal black tie event. Moana looks ravishing. She always does. Even in jeans and a t-shirt. Regin smiles at the picture of the two of them. He looks at the two pictures on the right of his desk. The first one is of his family. It is a photograph of Frea's junior high graduation. The second picture on the right is just of Frea. It is her grade ten school photograph. Regin smiles at them both. He looks at Frea on the right and then at Moana in the picture just next to it. She is her mother's daughter he thinks to himself. Though they are different by nature they are similarly beautiful.

There is a knock on the door. The person does not wait for Regin to respond. This is unusual. Only his peers or those from the C floor come in without waiting for the invitation. The knock is just courtesy. It is Christian Camael. He is dressed in black slacks with a white shirt and red tie. The tie is shockingly red. As red as blood that you might think he had been stabbed in the neck and the blood is gushing from an open wound and that it is not a tie at all. But Camael has not been stabbed in the neck. Though you might say that figuratively he has been stabbed in the back. Not by our man Regin. No. But by others on the board who have found him to be too soft. Too compassionate. And it is true that he is a compassionate and kind man. It is what everyone loves about him. Never in the history of Anzu Inc. have so many employees been so happy. But our man Regin is more malleable. You might say he is more agreeable to the powers that be.

Camael walks in with a smile on his face. He is a big man. He is not fat but he is big. He is six feet and three inches and solid as a linebacker. He played football in college. It was on a football scholarship. He is an imposing figure. Not handsome but rather plain. He has two children around Frea's age and a wife. He has been married almost as long as Regin. Regin stands up and smiles back at Christian. Christian is a difficult man to hate. You'd have to work at it pretty hard. You'd have to be pretty mean-spirited too. Good morning Christian says our man Regin. Good morning says Christian. Can I sit down he asks. Please says Regin. Christian takes a seat and then Regin follows. Regin frowns. Not at Christian. No. Christian is looking around the office. Regin frowns because he is not sure what to think of this unannounced visit. He has always liked Christian but they have never been chums. It is unusual for Christian to visit him in his office. It has only happened twice before in the seven years at this point that Christian has been CEO. It's been a good tenure. Profits have increased over ten percent per year during his reign. Same with sales. But as I said the board is not happy with him. They feel profits should be better. Sales should be better.

But perhaps more importantly they are worried about Christian apologizing for the Beirut Dilemma. He has already several times tried to put forth a motion to pay reparations and to accept liability for the people of Lebanon. But that will not do for the board. Not at all.

Regin is about to speak but Christian is first. The CEO's office is about four or five times larger wouldn't you say says Christian. His voice is warm. There is no hint of malice or of disappointment. In fact he smiles broadly at Regin. As if they were old friends. Christian does not know why Regin of all the VPs has been so reserved. Why Regin has kept himself at arm's distance from Christian. But Regin has always had his eye on the top job. And to befriend a man whose knees you'll be hoping to cut out from under him doesn't make Regin feel good. So he keeps a distance. What Regin doesn't know is that Christian would have been a good friend. A stellar ally. Especially in three years hence. When Regin's world is destroyed by butterfly wings. Indeed Christian did reach out. He tried to call. He sent his condolences. But Regin could not accept help. And that is a great pity and a deep sadness. There was much help to be had. And better decisions to be made. But Regin finds the milk of human kindness hard to swallow. Perhaps it is in his nature. His competitive spirit. It is also his error. But is it not the milk of human kindness that feeds the human spirit. That is not a rhetorical question. No. We both know the answer. If there is a commonality that all humans cherish it is this. Kindness. Children require it. Adults applaud it. Without it this world is solitary poor nasty brutish and short. That's from Leviathan. Its writer was Thomas Hobbes. Many of you may be familiar with that quote. Hobbes might have been hobbled by his times but he was right about that. Kindness makes the living bearable. Especially when it isn't. We are all broken. The glue of common courage made thick from the tears of pain keeps us together.

I trust your judgment says Regin. He smiles at Camael. He cannot help himself. Camael is a man who despite his imposing figure puts everyone at ease. You might call him a gentle giant. But he is not a giant. Though he is gentle. I'll take a look at the blueprints to be sure says Christian. He laughs loudly. Regin smiles more broadly. Regin is not sure what to do. What Christian wants. Can I get you a drink our man asks. It is not a real question. It is more a sound meant to fill the silence. To oil the discourse. Much like talking about the weather does the same. No no no says Christian. You might be wondering why I'm here he says. Regin nods his head. He tries not to be too vigorous about it. Though he is curious. Christian steadies his gaze on Regin. It is a soft gaze. The gaze of a confident man who has seen the deep sorrows of his fellow man. It is a gaze that you can get lost in. Where you see your hardships mirrored back. Only a little softer and less terrifying. I came to congratulate you says Christian. For what asks Regin. Christian laughs. You are a modest man says Christian. I don't think it is your modesty they are after though he adds. I have come to congratulate you on your promotion to CEO says Christian. I haven't heard anything announced officially says Regin. You have now says Christian. Regin looks at the man whose job he has just stolen. I didn't want it like this our man Regin says. There is no need for our man to deny his interest. It has become very apparent that Regin was one of the front runners early on. Not at all says Christian. Do not be dismayed he says. I am happy for you says Christian. My time has come and gone he says. I know they have made a good choice says Christian.

And he really believes that. Camael does believe it. Regin is the sort of man that the board wants. So they've made the right decision. Regin would have been Camael's first choice if he had been asked. He wasn't. I will do whatever I can to help you during the transition says Christian. Thank you says Regin.

You've always been very good like that he says. Christian smiles at him. How long will you be staying on asks Regin. Not long I'm afraid says Christian. The board wants a quick transition he says. But I am all yours until then he says. It likely won't be longer than a month he says. What Christian doesn't know is that the board doesn't want him to unduly influence Regin. Soften was the word one of the board members used. They don't want Christian to soften Regin. I'll be sorry to see you go says Regin. And he is sorry. As I've said before. Christian is a difficult man to hate. You'd really have to try. And there'd have to be something wrong with your own character. Christian has never committed a crime. Not even stolen a candy from a store. He doesn't speed. He always wears his seatbelt. He signals all the time. He is one of those rare individuals that just naturally do the right thing all the time. It's a delight to watch. He is the avant garde of the light brigade. Those of us fighting against the darkness. The darkness within our own breasts and the darkness that stains some of our souls. What are you hoping to do asks Regin. You are a young man yet he says. You are very kind says Christian. Though that is a little untrue. Regin is kind but he is not the very kind of kind. Not like Christian. If kindness were a sport then Christian would be MVP in the major leagues. Regin would be a bench warmer for the farm team. Kind Regin is. But he does not play at the level of kindness Christian does. My wife and I will be getting more fully involved in our commitment to children's charities says Christian. Anzu has been very good to me he says. Though that is a lie. They have used him until he was no longer useful. But the parachute he is getting is very generous. Let there be no doubt about that. When Chastity and Faith are both off at university says Christian we will devote our full time to our charities. I forget the name of your charities says Regin. He is trying to be polite but he is also interested. Love's Light Children's Cottages is the main one my wife and I founded says Christian. We bring in children who have been neglected and discarded he says. The little ones that nobody wants he says. Those are the ones we want he adds. Christian's eyes sparkle with light as he speaks about that which is most dear to him. With the generosity of Anzu I'll be able to open half a dozen cottages within the next few years says Christian. And God willing we'll be opening more as time goes by he adds. Regin is awestruck by this giant of a man. A man revered in the business world and who once covered the front pages of Forbes and BusinessWeek. I will ensure that Anzu Inc. remains a corporate sponsor so long as I have any say in it says Regin. That would be wonderful says Christian. And if you ever get the chance Mary and I would consider it an honor if you and Moana visited us at one of the cottages says Christian.

Regin is a little embarrassed that he has forgotten Christian's wife's name. But that is just how they differ. Well that's all I really wanted to say says Christian. I wanted to be the first to congratulate you Regin he says. They've chosen the best man for the job he adds. Christian stands up. Regin stands up with him. Christian extends his hand and they shake. By the way says Christian as he turns to go mum's the word until it's officially released by the board. That should happen tomorrow he says. Understood says Regin. Just before he closes the door Christian turns one last time towards Regin. I'll see you at lunch then he says. You bet says Regin. And with that Christian closes the door. Regin takes a moment to stare after him. Then he pumps his fist in the air. He will phone his wife. This promotion has been well earned and well deserved. He is thrilled. This is the culmination of a life's work and striving. He can't wait to sit in the big chair. Stand at the helm of the ship. Regin picks up the phone to dial home. There is a knock at the door. Regin looks at it and frowns. He sighs. This is frustrating for him. Yes he says more sternly than he meant. His secretary tentatively opens the door. She peeks her head in. She is an older woman. She wears gray. That is her favorite color. Her color of choice. It would be difficult to remember when her world was not shades of gray. Regin does not think of this but in the twelve years she has been his secretary he has never seen her wear a splash of color. The riskiest she's ever been with color is the occasional cream colored jersey. Otherwise it's gray. Today she wears a gray skirt that falls to mid calf. Her shoes are black. She doesn't own a brown pair. They have no heel. Her blouse is white and over top of it she wears a gray jacket. She is fifty-seven. She has never been married. Some would call her a spinster. But that is unkind. She was never interested. She lives in a one bedroom apartment in New Dorp Staten Island. This is not interesting. She has a cat. The cat is also gray. She lives simply. She invests her own money in the stock market and already has over three million dollars of investments. You'd never know it. She likes to knit. She belongs to a book club. When she's feeling splurgy she'll go and play bingo. Though that only happens once every few months. She wears cat eye style glasses with gray frames. She doesn't dye her hair. This means her hair is gray. She keeps it short and out of her face in a small bun at the back. She eats plain but healthy food and is in average shape. Though time has thickened her middle as it is wont to do.

You think you know her from my description but you don't. You're judging a book by its cover. You might think she is dour and perhaps brings to mind a tetchy old school marm. You'd be wrong. This would be your error. Veronica Allgoode. That is her name. She plays in the big leagues with Christian. The kindness big leagues. She is in the same league as Camael. Her savings will all go to two charities. Children's charities of which Camael's Love's Light Children's Cottages will be a big recipient. The other half will go to a selection of animal charities. Veronica will retire when she is seventy. A forced retirement from Anzu Inc. She will die peacefully in her sleep at ninety-seven. At that time she will leave over fifty million to her chosen charities. She lives simply. She does this because she believes in the words of Gandhi. To live simply so that others may simply live. Her other heroes include Mother Theresa. She is Catholic and attends Sunday morning mass religiously. She has never missed a Sunday mass in forty-seven years. As far back as she can reliably remember.

I am sorry Mr. Sigurd she says peeking her head round the door. I don't mean to intrude she says. Regin likes her. She has been his secretary for twelve years. Ever since he came back from the Beirut Dilemma. She is reliable punctual and brilliant at her job. She is probably the best assistant anyone at Anzu has. That's a small lie. She is the best. Regin smiles at her and puts down the phone. No no not at all he says to Veronica. Please come and sit down V he says waving at one of the chairs across from his desk. Veronica comes in and sits down. What can I help you with he asks her. Well she says. I just saw Mr. Camael leave and I was wondering if you've heard any news yet she says. She smiles warmly at him. Though she is only eight years older than him she feels motherly towards him. She likes to take care of him and that is what makes her so successful at her job. Well I can't really say he says. Regin smiles at her. If there is one other person in the world from whom he has never kept secrets it is his assistant Veronica Allgoode. The other woman being his wife of course. Indeed in many ways Veronica has been like a confidant. I understand she says smiling at him. I have already called Mr. Mara to pick you up at eleven forty she says. This is an important day for you Mr. Sigurd and I should think that punctuality is the best course on such an auspicious day she says. Regin smiles. I think you are right he says. It is an auspicious day he adds. I know I have always been able to trust you he adds. You have been the most trustworthy person I know besides my wife he says. Thank you she says. I have always wanted you to excel she says. Regin nods. So I will let you in on a little secret he says. Christian was just here to congratulate me in person on the promotion to CEO he says. Veronica smiles broadly and claps her hands and holds them to her bosom. I am so happy for you Mr. Sigurd she says. I know you have wanted it for a very long time she says. And you are most deserving of it she adds. Thank you V says our man. But please keep this under wraps until it is officially announced through the appropriate channels he says. Of course she says. You are the first one to know says Regin. I have not yet even had the chance to call my wife he says. Then please excuse me says Veronica. I will let you get right to that she says. Veronica stands up and beams broadly at Regin. Congratulations she says. This is the best news I've heard in years she says. Thank you says Regin. Veronica leaves his office and closes the door. Regin picks up the phone again and calls his wife. You can imagine how happy she is. Not much more is needed for me to add here.

Yama Mara is waiting patiently for our man Regin at eleven thirty. Ten minutes later Regin exits the building. Yama with his spindly fingers opens the rear passenger door. Thank you says Regin. It is my great pleasure says Yama. Though that is a lie. He takes no pleasure in being servile. Yama rounds the car and gets into the driver's seat. He pulls out into traffic. He starts towards the best steak restaurant in the city. I could name it for you but I won't. Some of the minutiae is extraneous to the story I'm telling. The details that matter are the errors our man Regin makes. Not where he eats or the specific address of his home or work. You get the idea. If you want an idea of the sort of place he's going to. It's in the top ten of any list of the best steakhouses in New York. It is also one of the most expensive ones. You'll need at least a Benjamin to pay for each guest. Enough said.

Have you brought an appetite with you sir asks Yama. It is an odd question. But behind it is a hidden meaning. Yama is wondering if Regin is hungry for success. If he is willing to spin his compass. The moral one. In order to attain the trappings of wealth and success. Regin is. He is not willing to be wholly immoral. But he is willing to bend a little on the details. These are his errors. You will see this soon enough. The Beirut Dilemma is where it all started. The slippery slope if you will of Regin's downfall. I am always hungry for good food says our man Regin. Yama smiles. I am sure today is a very good day for you sir he says. You haven't heard anything yet have you asks Yama. Regin looks at Yama's beady black eyes in the rearview mirror. We know Regin has heard. But Yama is not one of the people he would trust with this confidence. Regin has not just fallen off the turnip truck. Regin does not mind lying. Not when it is a small lie like this next one is. No he says. I have not heard anything in the definitive yet he adds. And although this is a lie it is not a major one. The word of Camael as the CEO is not the definitive word on his promotion. That has to come from the board. And it is the Chairman of the Board who will deliver the news. And it must come with a contract. Then it is definitive. I am certain it is yours says Yama grinning like the all knowing Cheshire cat. I appreciate your confidence says Regin. The journey to the restaurant is quick. It only takes ten minutes. The rest of the way Yama and Regin sit in silence. This is what Regin prefers. He does not enjoy banter with Yama. As I have said before there is something about Yama that is off-putting. They arrive at the front of the restaurant at eleven fifty. Yama gets out and opens the door for Regin. I will wait here for you sir says Yama. Thank you says Regin. Our man Regin walks up to the front door of the restaurant as Yama bores into the back of his head. Yama's mind is mulling over the future. How our man Regin might be able to bring him wealth and prestige that he feels he deserves.

Regin enters the restaurant and tells the maître d' his purpose. Your company has already arrived says the maître d'.

Please come this way he says. The maître d' is dressed in a tuxedo. He is an older man. He is sixty-three. He is a bachelor. Never married. None of this is important. I am just trying to add flavor to the tale. He is of average height. His hair is thinning and gray. Though he dies it black. It is brushed back. He wears a pencil thin mustache that is closely cropped. He has a small belly on thin legs. He likes to drink. You can see it in his nose and cheeks. Splintered burst spidery veins and a ruddy complexion. He holds a white napkin over his left forearm. This is just for show. He does nothing with it. At a private corner of the restaurant sit six members of the board of Anzu Inc. as well as the Chairman of the Board who is Anzu Buer. The board has one woman and one person of color. That person is one and the same. This is the type of company that Anzu Inc. is. They are not progressive. Though they like to think they are. This woman is Tariro Chiweshe. She was born in Zimbabwe. Though at that time it was known as Rhodesia. None of this is important. Though Tariro goes by Tari. She is not present at this meeting. She is a board member by name. Nobody defers to her much though everyone is polite. This is how prejudice is covered by the cloak of civility. Nevertheless this is not a tale about racism and prejudice. Though that is one of humanity's greatest errors. The cause of much of our suffering. But let us get back to the task at hand. Anzu Buer stands up. He is sitting at the head of the table. Regin walks up to him and shakes his hand. Good afternoon sir he says. It is not afternoon but he can be forgiven. It is eleven fifty-three. This too is not important. Each side of the table has four chairs. The first three on each side starting from the head seat the board members. Regin says good afternoon to the other board members. Then he sits down opposite Christian Camael. This has been done purposefully. Christian stands just before Regin sits and they shake hands. Anzu Buer is pleased with all this fake civility. Though he does not realize that it is not fake.

The waiter comes by. He is not dressed in a tuxedo though he wears a black bow tie a white shirt and black pants. His shoes are black polished to a mirror finish. Around his waist he wears a white apron. It is virgin white. Unmarked by the carnage of blood and offal that this restaurant serves. Any suggestion of the violence involved in these meals is never shown. Nobody wants to dine on the flesh of dead beasts while aware of their suffering. Discretion in this instance is the better part of cowardice. But this is not a morality tale about the violence we commit against innocents. No. This is a morality tale about choices and the errors we make. Not the least of which is the errors in our choices when it comes to compassion. With the beasts we heap burdens upon as well as amongst our own brethren. But let us stick just with the errors amongst brethren. The waiter takes the orders. Our man Regin orders the porterhouse steak. Everyone else orders meat of some sort. None of them would think otherwise. Anzu Buer orders a couple of bottles of the finest red wine. This meal will come to over two thousand dollars when it is all said and done. This is not even a line item in petty cash. The talk is about current events. Some of it political. This is a table of conservatives. Republicans mostly. Though some are leaning a little more to the right. This is also their error. The world is a somewhat vile place because men and women care not for their fellow men and women. Conservatives are more prone to this error than others. Nevertheless it is the capitalist system which continues this fault line upon which our social fabric continues to quake.

But this too is not a political tale. Though I suppose it is all of these things. All of these choices are breadcrumbs upon our journey to the witch's cottage. But lest this turn into a tome of great length I will try to limit my focus upon the choices of our man Regin. He is choosing steak. And already his arteries are rotting from cholesterol and sores caused by this rich diet of his. It would be enough to kill him off in time. But that does not happen. We know it. Though he would have been dead by sixty if he had continued on this perverse diet. The chit chat remains superficial. The waiter comes by with the red wine. He pours some for Anzu who is clearly the man at the helm. Anzu is satisfied. So each of them is poured a half glass. The red wine is thick and dark like pooled blood. Regin likes it. On the table the waiter places crusty warm white buns. They are fresh and doughy. Freshly churned butter is placed beside each basket of bread. The men help themselves to the bread. Not all of them. But our man Regin does. He spreads a lavish smear of butter on each side of the bun he has torn in half. The butter starts to soften and melt on the warm guts of the bread. Regin takes a bite. The bun is crunchy and soft and chewy on the inside. Our man Regin doesn't realize how hungry he is. Everyone defers to Anzu to lead the conversation. But he will not start talk of the changing of the guard before they are well into their meals. He talks to those board members nearest him about the stock price. It has drifted sideways for the last year. Hovering in the range of seventy to eighty dollars a share. Recent guidance that Camael has given on the advice of the board puts a hundred dollar price tag on the share by the end of the next fiscal year. It will get there. Because Regin will do the difficult decisions that Camael would not. He will fire thousands. He will slash at costs. But perhaps more importantly without Regin's input the general economy will improve and a rising tide lifts all boats. Though Regin will get the acknowledgement for the success. He will be richly rewarded. Unjustly so. I say this because it is true. Not because I am purposefully being contrarian. Very little success of a business resides on the CEO. The giant's share of success in any company comes from middle management and below. But this is not an economics tale. There is talk of splitting the stock price when it gets to one hundred dollars. There is no doubt in these men's minds that the price will not get there. And there is general agreement that the price will get there. Most of this is not important. It is just filler. Like the buns on the table. Tasty morsels that offer no real sustenance.

The waiter comes by again and starts to place white china in front of the guests. Burnt flesh mostly from bovines is offered in supplication for these men's sins. Though that's like putting gasoline on a fire. What they need is what Esau sold his birthright for. Pottage of lentils and vegetables. Esau was a coarse and unrefined man. Our man Regin does not have this excuse. But at least Esau knew what a good meal was. But I digress. These plates being served by the waiter are generous in burnt flesh but stingy with anything that might offer a semblance to plants. But that does not bother these men. Their eyes dwell upon the thickness and size of bovine muscles. They are well pleased as they lick their chops. Nobody starts eating until everyone has been served. As it happens Anzu is served last. But this is of no consequence. The waiter whose name incidentally is Jacob asks if there is anything else needed. Anzu declines. Jacob bows himself away. Anzu picks up the bottle of wine and tops up the glasses of those close to him. Following his lead Camael does the same at the other end. Anzu raises his glass. The rest follow like supplicant docile sheep. To the changing of the guard says Anzu Buer looking around at his men like a benevolent general. And it gives Anzu great pleasure to think of himself as a benevolent man. And he believes it. Though the truth is not as generous. Everyone clinks glasses. Regin and Christian lock eyes for a moment. Camael nods at our man in acknowledgement. Please eat says Anzu and we will get to the business end of this lunch in a minute. They tuck in. The meal is good. This restaurant has earned its place at the top honestly. If honesty can be aligned with murder and the butchering of innocents. I use the vernacular murder carefully. We indulgent humans like children think only of ourselves when thinking upon murder. Yet it is proper to consider the act of killing murder even when it comes to our younger siblings who share not our form nor voice. The meal lives up to the expectations of those paying. Paying a single mother's monthly salary for one meal shared between eight men. But let us not dwell on these injustices at the moment. This is part of the tale that is celebratory. This is the part that our man Regin has longed for.

As the carcasses are carried away the conversation turns to the matter at hand. Port has been ordered now that the wine has been drained. It is served with assorted cheeses and fruit. Only the finest. We all know why we are here says Anzu Buer. We are here to elect our newest Chief Executive Officer he says. And that man will be Regin Sigurd he says. Anzu looks right chuffed. He raises his glass towards Regin. Regin raises his in turn. There is no one more qualified Anzu says. And there is no one who brings greater experience to this table than Regin he adds. I am certain that under his new direction Anzu will see greater success than it has in a long time says Anzu. This is a small slight towards Camael but Camael does not notice. He is not one to take offense at the spite from small minds. If truth be told and I am wont to do it. Then Camael is somewhat relieved he will be able to move forward in the next chapter of his life. A life that will be of service. That brings him great pleasure. Christian Camael continues Anzu has served Anzu Incorporated diligently and professionally for his tenure. We are very grateful for your services Christian says Anzu lifting his glass up to him. Christian returns the gesture. It has been my honor and pleasure he says. This he means. It has been a pleasure and honor for him. Everyone is feeling smug and self important. Perhaps this cannot be helped. These are men after all who believe their work is important. It is not. No. Not really. But they are paid king's ransoms and that makes it feel like important work. Nay. In many ways some of them feel they are doing God's work. Though that is the height of human hubris. But one cannot sway another man's sentiment easily. And worse still there is no one here to sway it.

I am pleased says Anzu that the board's decision was unanimous in recommending you for the position of Chief Executive. Anzu is looking at Regin. Regin is looking at Anzu. They look at each other like tentative lovers. Regin admires the man. In fact he likes him. But there is something about him that causes discomfort in his being. You might say that Anzu is like the princess's pea. The one stuck in her mattress. Perhaps a better analogy is that Anzu is like the parasite caught in the oyster. The pearl an immune response of self preservation. Though I reach to suggest that Regin is a pearl. He is not. But neither is he a scoundrel. But Anzu is a fickle and fair-weather friend. So long as the weather is fair he is your friend. What is meant by this is easy to understand. If you do as Anzu wishes you have a friend. If not. Then you're in a world of hurt. Intuitively and subconsciously Regin understands this. But he is not evolved enough to accept it consciously. This is part of his errors. Regin is unable to swim in the murky depths of his soul. Where the monsters lie. As such he gives them greater nourishment from which to grow. Though he still never sees them. Is never able to conquer them. The shareholders' vote was not unanimous says Anzu grinning. There is an eruption of laughter like the bursting of a boil. Regin chuckles too. But then again says Anzu nothing that shareholders vote on is ever unanimous. A small difficulty that we have to deal with he says. We will announce it officially tomorrow with a press release says Anzu. We wanted to bring you here today to make it official to you says Anzu. Tomorrow you will take the helm from Christian he says. Anzu looks at Regin for a while. He does not say anything. He waits. Patient as a spider for a fly to fling itself against his web. Regin clears his throat. This is a great honor he says. I know I will do you proud he adds. Anzu nods. I know you will says the spider to the fly. For Anzu is like a spider that feasts on the bodies of those that work for him. Regin would have found this out if he had lasted long enough. But he does not. Christian is ousted because he would not let the parasite feast on his innards. Anzu managed one good deed in his life. He saved Adelmo. But a life is not made of one good deed. It takes a lifetime of them to align the soul.

At the end of the lunch. When the bellies of the wolves are full. When they have satiated themselves on the death of others. Then it is time for the real business. The business of Regin selling his soul to the devil. Our man Regin does this easily and happily. It is nothing to him for he sees little consequence in becoming the CEO. This is his error. One that he will not come to learn from. For he is dead too soon. Perhaps that was a small kindness. Though it is hard to call death a kindness. At least under these circumstances. Regin signs eagerly. He celebrates his success with sex with his wife that very same evening. She is compliant. He is now the alpha male. Though his master might as well be the devil himself. He dominates her though she is unaware of his dominion. He is oblivious too. But this is how it is. Be careful what you wish for a wise man once said. It might have been Goethe. That's not important. Though great literature can teach us much. It is better to learn from other's troubles than one's own. The cost of that school is cheap. The quality of education superior. But for our own errors we choose to err on the side of excess. Let us leave our man Regin. This is a momentous occasion for him. One in which he feels important. It is important. For it is the culmination of a long line of errors. He does not know this. But he comes to understand. Indeed he comes to understand deeply. But right now he is happy. How sad this is. How sad his miserable little life has become. And he remains blighted by the false bliss of ignorance. Much like the orgasm at the hands of a hooker. How empty and vacuous. How hollow and wanting the soul still feels. Do not judge me for being harsh. If nothing else nobody was harsh enough. For the errors of our man Regin compounded upon themselves. Like a snowball falling down a steep mountain face. And here it is. Our man Regin will lie dead. Because he would not foresee the monsters in his head. A rhyme makes it sound sublime. No. Let us go then. Let us leave Regin on this false summit of joy. For the valley is deep and the valley is dark. And dug it with his own hands.

The Beginning

Gentle reader. You are kind to have come so far with me on this treacherous tale. A traitorous tale in many ways. One's own heart the traitor maker. We have moved further back in time in our story. When last we were together. We were witness to Regin's promotion. The lofty height from which he would soon fall. That would happen three years hence. Now we are even further back in time. Regin is a much younger man. Our man is a gentle thirty-seven. His wife though no more is at this time thirty-five. His dear daughter. Little Frea is only four. It is a hot and dry summer in Lebanon. Life is next to idyllic for our man and his family. Regin is in Beirut. Anzu Inc. has just opened up a refinery in the outskirts of Beirut. We are fifteen years in the past. Remember dear reader this story starts at the end. From the end. From that prison cell we are fifteen years in the past. What a difference a few years makes. Would you not agree. Yes. Our man Regin has recently started his family. He almost feels complete. He has a good job. He has a beautiful wife who loves him. He has a daughter. The apple of his eye. He is paid well. He has traveled the world. Not literally. But he has seen good bits of it. He has the world at his feet. And he is about to fuck it up. Forgive the strong language. You see. Already at this stage he has his eyes set on the prize. The prize is the CEO's office. The incumbent is the man who started it all. Anzu Buer is still in charge. He will not retire for a few years. Five to be precise. But everyone knows it's coming. The old man is getting older. There is no favored man found yet who will take the reigns. These soon to be red reigns. You will come to understand this metaphor. We are about to be witness to the Beirut Dilemma. All on our man Regin's watch.

You are about to become acquainted with what a catastrophe this Beirut Dilemma is. But it needn't have been such. It should have been different. This is the fulcrum. This is the fulcrum from which Regin's world is about to be sent into an orbit of chaos from which he will not escape. That word fulcrum is interesting. No. It comes from the Latin which means to literally prop up. This Beirut Dilemma. It is where his world is propped up only to come crashing down. Such a tragedy. And it never need be. It should have not happened. But this is the nature of human avarice and greed. We take shortcuts to fill the coffers. Coffers comes from the Latin and old French for small box or basket. Is it not irony that coffin comes from the same root. I think it is not. These are not venial sins. Venial sins do not deprive the soul of divine grace. Mortal sins do deprive the soul. And yet avarice and greed are not mortal sins either. At least not according to Catholic doctrine. Our man Regin is not Catholic. But the Protestants have similar feelings about sin. This greed and avarice. Really one and the same. Twin brothers. These are part of the heptad. The heptad of deadly sevens. They are neither venial nor mortal but only ascribed as such upon the circumstance. This circumstance. This Beirut Dilemma makes them mortal. Though this does not say much. No. Not when masturbation is considered a mortal sin. This is the problem with dogma. And dogma is always aligned with religion. And religion is always bent towards man's interpretation. In any event. This Beirut Dilemma is the coffin that our man Regin makes for himself. You will see soon enough. Regin did not oversee the construction. He came to Lebanon to run the show once it was built. But how he handled it. This was his gravest error. This was his cardinal sin. The sin from which all the others were born. Like a budding plant. This was the root that gave blossom to his downfall. You will see dear reader how this happened. Where most of this current portion of the tale takes place is after Regin has been here for some time. Indeed this is his one hundredth and sixty-seventh day in Lebanon. The refinery has been working well for many months. It is at full capacity. But there is a chink in the armor.

But first let us look at the day before. Let us visit Fadi Hajjar and his family. Little Fadi is four years old. He is the apple of his father's eye. This might sound familiar. It is meant to be. This is the similarity between Ashfaq and our man Regin. Ashfaq is Fadi's father. Ashfaq loves his job. He has just this past week been promoted to foreman. He is in charge of thirteen men. He is not paid well. But he is paid well by Lebanese standards. For every job on offer at Anzu Inc. in Beirut there are over one hundred applicants. This is a job with prestige. Ashfaq is well respected in his community. He is not a bad man. He is a devout and humble Muslim. As is his wife. She is Layla. This is an Arabic name. Though you would be forgiven for mistaking it for an English one. How egocentric we are. This is also our error. There is much that the Arabic world contributed to humanity's enlightenment. Along with the Greeks we owe a debt to the Arabs for mathematics. But this is not a tale of Arabic enlightenment and civilization. No. This is a tale of woe. Of our man Regin. But I must interject occasionally. You will forgive me for adding flavor. This is important. It is important we be reminded that our blood is red. That beneath the different shades of skin life courses through our veins in red. You see

Ashfaq dote upon his son. You see Regin dote upon his daughter. You see the love in Layla's eyes for Fadi and Ashfaq. You see the love in Moana's. We see the common human experience. We are all the same. The letter inside the envelope speaks of love and justice and joy and hope. The languages may differ but the yearning is the same. Ashfaq is Regin as Regin is Ashfaq. This is the intertwined fabric upon which we are just interlaced threads. Let us not mistake the wrapping for the content. For the content is the same even though the wrapping is not.

Ashfaq has come home from work. He walks with the other men down the dusty road towards home. The bus has dropped them off. In his hand he carries a small cloth bag. In it was his lunch. Now eaten. In his other hand he carries a hard hat. His face is dirty and sweat stained. His black mustache well trimmed. Fadi and Layla are in the home. It is a small home with two bedrooms. But it is theirs. It will not be Layla's in a short time. It will be taken from her. She will move back home with Fadi to live with her parents. Otherwise she would be destitute. But this is to come. Now she stands in the kitchen cooking shish taouk. This is marinated chicken on skewers. Down the road the men including Ashfaq can smell the scents from the kitchen. The men's mouths water. It has been a long day. The work is laborious. Layla is preparing a garlic paste for the chicken called toum. The tabbouleh and hummus is ready. These are Ashfaq's favorite foods. They are Fadi's too. Fadi hears the door open. Daddy he says. He was just sitting by his mother on the kitchen floor playing with an American toy car. He gets up and runs to the door. Ashfaq kneels. He puts the hard hat and bag down. He grabs Fadi and lifts him up into his arm. He kisses him on the forehead. I missed my beautiful boy he says. He is not speaking English. You know this. He is speaking Arabic. Though he is fluent in French and English. Fadi only speaks Arabic. Layla is trilingual like her husband. None of this is important. The love they have amongst them is. Ashfaq carries his son in the crook of his right arm. His son has his arms around his father's neck. It is a touching scene. You can imagine. What did you do today asks Ashfaq. Fadi pulls his head back from his father's neck. He has his arms around his father still. I played outside says Fadi. I played with my truck and I played with my car he says. You are a good boy says Ashfaq. And he is a good boy. But he will grow up to be an angry young man. We know this. We have seen it. We have seen Fadi's anger and its consequences. We have seen the blood he spilled. Mixed amongst his own. But let us not dwell on the future. Remember. We are moving backwards. So that we might learn. Might take the lessons and make better choices. It is not too late for us. For Regin and Fadi. For Ashfaq and Frea. All of these choices are mute. The dice have been cast. The debts already repaid. But our ledger is clean. We might yet learn to live in the black.

Ashfaq carries Fadi into the kitchen. Layla looks up from the pan. She smiles at her husband. Her hard working husband. With this sweat stained shirt and neatly trimmed black mustache. My husband she says. Did you have a good day she asks. I worked hard says Ashfaq. He comes over and kisses her on the mouth. She tastes sweet. It is in the lip gloss on her lips. He tastes salty. It is the hard work. The salty sweat that has dried on his lips. Ashfaq puts Fadi back down on the floor. How long for dinner asks Ashfaq. Fifteen minutes my love says Layla. I will go and wash up he says. Ashfaq leaves the kitchen to go to the bathroom. One bathroom in this house. But it is theirs. It also has a shower and a bath. This is the envy of the neighbors. Fadi walks out and follows his father. Fadi says Layla a little sternly. Fadi stops. He turns around to look at his mother. In his hand is the American car. It is a red Camaro. It is a replica of the sixty-seven Camaro. It hangs from his hand like a bulbous clot of blood. Earlier Fadi was dirty. He had been playing outside like he told his father. But Layla had cleaned him up before she started dinner. She had given him a bath. Fadi is now in pajamas. He wears pajama shorts and a short buttoned shirt. It is in light cotton. It is printed with Winnie the Pooh and Tigger. Fadi does not know these characters. Not yet. Neither his mother nor father have read him the stories of Winnie the Pooh. Daddy needs to wash up says Layla. Let Daddy have a few minutes to himself she says. Fadi looks at his mother. She smiles at him. She is not angry. Fadi's lower lip quivers and turns upside down. But I want Daddy says little Fadi. Layla puts the spoon down and goes up to Fadi. She kneels down to his height. Little Fadi's lip is quivering like a caterpillar on a windblown leaf. His eyes are brimming with bright tears. Layla takes him into her arms. Daddy wants you too she says into his ear. Just give Daddy five minutes she says. He will be back out in just a moment she adds. Don't be sad she says. Daddy loves you she says. You'll see she adds Daddy will be out very soon. Fadi does not cry. Okay he says in his small voice clogged with emotion. Layla goes back to the stove and picks up the spoon. Show me how fast your car goes she says to Fadi. Fadi comes over and kneels down on one knee. He takes the red car and pushes it off towards the other end of the kitchen. It crashes into the dining room table's leg. That's very fast says Layla. Fadi scurries after it. How sensitive my son is thinks Layla. And he is. It is the sensitive ones for which the world is not made. It is these gentle spirits that the world bruises more easily. We've seen how this goes. This does not end well. We must all be careful to do the right thing. Not like our man Regin. Not like tomorrow. Not how he handles the Beirut Dilemma. There are three people in this house. One of them will not come home tomorrow. We know who that is. But let us not get ahead of ourselves.

Ashfaq is not late out of the shower. He dresses in beige slacks and a white shirt. This is not his regular uniform. No. For work he wears blue coveralls. Those are now in the laundry hamper for Layla to take care of. Layla is putting plates of food on the table. Ashfaq is hungry. The work is hard and the days are long. The house smells delicious. He comes back into the kitchen. Sit husband says Layla. Let me feed you she says. She smiles at him. Fadi comes and sits down next to his father. He sits on a tall cushion. His chin not far above the table. Layla serves up her husband first. The shish taouk is not on skewers for Fadi. She has cut the pieces up into bite-sized pieces of chicken for Fadi. The toum is on the side for dipping. On the side of his plate. Also on his plate is tabbouleh. Ashfaq's plate only carries two skewers of chicken. A large bowl of tabbouleh and another bowl of hummus are in the middle of the table. A smaller bowl in the middle of the table holds toum for Layla and Ashfaq. Layla comes and sits down opposite her husband. Ashfaq closes his eyes and says a prayer for the blessings he has received and for the food. Layla does the same. Bismillah says Ashfaq. Bismillah says Layla. Ashfaq puts his red Camaro next his plate. Ashfaq looks at it. But he does not say anything. He rustles his son's black hair. Black as his own. Fadi looks up and smiles at his father. Eat says Ashfaq to his son. Eat so that you will grow big and strong like your father he says. Ashfaq's hair is still damp from the shower. It makes him look handsome thinks Layla. But it also makes her feel sad. It is the color of his patent leather shoes he wore to his own father's funeral. That was just after Fadi was born. Layla looks away at her plate. Ashfaq pulls of a piece of chicken from the skewer with his fork. He dips it in the toum. He eats it. He smiles at his wife. You make me happy he says. You have cooked my favorite meal and you have made it better than ever he says. Layla blushes almost embarrassedly. She bats her eyelids involuntarily. Thank you my darling she says. I like to make you happy she says. They eat in silence for a little while. I have some good news says Ashfaq. He looks from his son to his wife and from his wife to his son again. He points at Fadi's red car. We will have a car next year says Ashfaq. We will be able to drive in the countryside he says. Fadi looks up at his father. Like this one he asks. He points at his red Camaro. Similar says Ashfaq. Next summer we will visit Baalbeck he says. We will see the Temple of Bacchus and the Temple of Jupiter and the Great Stones he says. Layla smiles at her husband. I have only ever seen photographs she says. Ashfaq smiles. He looks at his son. We will have a picnic he says. We will make a day out of it he says. You are not just saying this asks his wife. No says Ashfaq. Today I found out my new salary he says. I will be paid twenty-five percent more than I was before he says. Ashfaq is proud. And he is smiling. We will have everything we want he says. That is not entirely true. Ashfaq exaggerates. But it will allow them a modest middle class lifestyle. They will be able to afford a car. Not a new one. But in a year he will be able to afford a used one.

Layla reaches her hand out across the table towards her husband. He takes it and squeezes it. This is very good news she says. You have worked hard for it and you deserve it she says. Ashfaq nods his head. And you have been very patient my wife he says. You have stood by me like a good wife all these years when times were lean he says. As is my duty she says. But not just your duty he adds. She smiles at him. No my husband she says not just my duty. They get back to eating the dinner. When Ashfaq has finished his chicken he piles tabbouleh and hummus onto his plate. He eats the tabbouleh with his fork. The hummus he scoops up with pita. Ashfaq asks about his son's day. Fadi tells him about everything that he did. When dinner is finished Layla takes the plates away to wash them. Ashfaq and Fadi move to the couch in the dining room. With wooden blocks they outline a racetrack. Fadi and Ashfaq race Fadi's cars around the track. Fadi uses the red Camaro. Fadi gives his father a blue Dodge Challenger. It is a ninety-seventy model. The Dodge Challenger cannot win the race. It seems the red Camaro is too fast. This is what Ashfaq tells his son. His son is proud. He smiles. This is Ashfaq letting his son win. This is the love of the father for his son. Ashfaq sometimes overtakes Fadi's car. But he cannot win. This is Ashfaq building his son's confidence and self-esteem. This is how it should be. Men should never compete with their children. It is their duty to lift them higher. Let them see beyond what they are capable of. At eight thirty in the evening Ashfaq takes Fadi to his room. He tucks him in. Layla looks in from the doorway. Then she retires to the living room. Ashfaq reads him a children's story. He reads it in Arabic. Fadi will learn English when he starts school. And he will learn French then too. Ashfaq sits on the side of the bed until Fadi has fallen asleep. Then he retires to the living room and sits with his wife.

Husband she says. Ashfaq looks at her. He does not like it when she starts a conversation that way. It usually means trouble. Yes he says. What has come of the safety concerns she asks. She speaks of the safety of the refinery. It is well known among the workers that Anzu Inc. has taken short cuts. This was brought to the attention of management through Ashfaq's predecessor. His name is Faruq. He does not work for Anzu anymore. You know why. Anzu Inc. has little tolerance for independent thought and criticism from its employees. Our man Regin fired him. Regin was pressured to. This is how spineless our man can be. This is why he will be chosen as CEO. Our man Regin is easy to control. He is easy to steer in the right direction. They know about the problems says Ashfaq. He does not want to talk about this. Do they know because you told them or because Faruq did asks Layla. Both says Ashfaq. Ashfaq wants to listen to the radio. He does not want to talk about the troubles at work. What did you say to them asks Layla. Ashfaq sighs. You do not understand my wife that I must walk carefully here he says. I told Mr. Boucher the same that Faruq told him says Ashfaq. And what did you tell him asks Layla. Her tone is soft but probing. She does not wish to anger her husband but she is worried about his safety. I told him that we did not believe the pipes and the welding were strong enough for the pressures put upon them he says. You know this he adds. Ashfaq is starting to get angry. And what did Mr. Boucher say asks Layla. That is enough says Ashfaq. Like he told Faruq the company is aware of the issue says Ashfaq. I am just worried for you she says. I do not mean to upset you husband she adds. You have he says. His voice is strained with controlled anger. You know what happened to Faruq he says. Do you wish for me to be jobless like him he asks. And then what will become of us he says. Layla shakes her head. Of course not my darling she says. Then let it be he says. He takes her hand in his. Mr. Boucher told me not to worry about it he says. He also told me that if I continued to worry about it that they would give me something else to worry about he adds. They would give me unemployment to worry about says Ashfaq. You know how many men want any of the jobs at Anzu he says. We need this job he says. We will ask Allah to watch over us says Ashfaq. I will take all the precautions I can he says. Trying to assuage his wife's fears. She smiles at him. Thin as the fabric on their used sofa. I know she says. I just worry she says. Do not worry he says. He is tired. He wants to listen to the radio. They do not yet have a television. That is something else he is saving for. I will be careful he says. He lets her hand go. He puts his hand on the side table. It is near the radio. He is ready to listen to it. The job pays well Ashfaq says. We will have a car and we will travel far he says. Do not worry my sweet wife he says. The best is yet to come he adds. He is a liar. But he does not know he lies. He believes in this bright future. But it is not his to determine.

Let us leave Ashfaq to listen to his radio. Let us leave him to sit with his obedient and loving wife. Let us leave him with his beloved son Fadi sound asleep in his bed. For this is their last night together. We will turn now to our man Regin. He has a nice house in Beirut. It is in the best suburb. According to expats in any event. It is on the outskirts of Beirut. Not far from the refinery. It is a gated community. Only management from the many European and American companies live here. Regin's house is over twenty-five hundred square feet. He has a cook and a cleaner. He is a big deal here. In Anzu he is just another upper management peon. But soon he will be on the fast track. He will soon be the Vice President of International Development. It looked like our man would be here for a while. Tomorrow is his one hundred and sixty-seventh day in Lebanon. Regin does not know this. He does not count the days. He quite likes it. He likes the Lebanese people. He likes their culture and their food. Even though he does not understand their religion. They work hard. They are friendly and respectful. These are many of the things he likes. After ninety days Moana joined him here. She misses cooking. Regin tells her to be respectful. They are providing work for a Lebanese woman. She is making her family wealthier. This is how Regin thinks. Moana thinks it is too posh. That is the word she uses. She likes that word. She spends her days with other women from Europe and Britain. It is the British women who gave her that word. How posh they'd say. These women impress Moana with their colonialism. She is not impressed by them. Rather they impress upon her their colonial views. Moana feels that the British in particular. But also the French. They seem unburdened by the opulence they show in contrast to their surroundings. They carry it with ease. They feel entitled. Their colonial attitude seems to subsume their own importance. One might even suggest they are racist. That they believe in the superiority of their own race. But that would be incorrect. Not only because they are outwardly polite. But also because racism as applied to race cannot be defined. Most prejudice is based upon phenotype which is not necessarily aligned with genotype or race. Yet this is not a treatise about racism. But Moana is not incorrect in feeling the snobbery of her peers. Especially the British and the French. Indeed these women believe themselves superior. They feel superior because they are wealthier. They feel superior because of their whiter skin. They are prejudiced because of their belief in a certain phenotype. But perhaps more so because of their classism. You might assume them to be xenophobic. But this would be your error. These women enjoy visiting other countries. It is not the people of other countries they fear or dislike. No. They are pleasant. They just think they are better. This is the problem with wealth. More specifically this is the problem with wealth disparity. The poor are always prejudiced against. It does not matter their phenotype or culture. It is their poverty against which we snub them.

Moana does not like this aspect of her peers. She does not feel comfortable with it. But of course it is all hidden from view. Everyone is superficially pleasant. Even amongst themselves these women do not remark snidely about the Lebanese. No. It is in their manner and their expressions. Moana is not like them. Within ninety days she will be glad to be back in the States. Though she will always carry the guilt for her husband. To be sure. He will carry some himself. But his conscience will be assuaged by others. It will also be put to ease by money. Lots of it. And of course a total lack of culpability. Moana will carry the guilt of the deaths of the many. The nine hundred and thirty that died. But we get ahead of ourselves. First we must join Moana and Regin as they finish dinner. It is interesting to note that they dine on shish taouk. The same meal as Ashfaq and Layla. Though this is not their last meal. It is Ashfaq's final dinner. Though he does not know it. That they eat the same meal is coincidence. Do not read more into it. There are things that are just coincidence. This is not a conspiracy. Shish taouk is a popular Lebanese dish. We must not be quick to see conspiracies under every coincidence. We must be quick however to see the results of our daily choices. These are the errors that Regin does not learn from. This is what causes his downfall. A failure of foresight. Indeed many will consider the Beirut Dilemma a conspiracy. As much as some consider Three Mile Island and Chernobyl a conspiracy. Perhaps even Bhopal. But the Beirut Dilemma. Just like these others is not a conspiracy. Human beings are too volatile to commit conspiracies at any large degree. No. What we see as conspiracy is nothing more than self interest. People with similar self interests will work together in those interests. This is what happens. This is what will happen with the Beirut Dilemma. But this is not what it is known as outside of Anzu Inc. No. Upon the global stage it is known as the Beirut Accident. But make no mistake. There is nothing accidental about it. Accidents happen due to human error. And let us count the ways. No. It would take too long. But rest assured there were plenty of human errors. Life would be a farce if it weren't so tragic. The errors we make. Like navel-gazing babies. All the world is a piece of lint. These are our errors. Our communal and our individual errors. Let us hope that you dear reader may take a lesson from this tragedy. From our man Regin's misfortune. Though that is the wrong word. Rather let us call it Regin's astigmatism. An astigmatism of the mind. For it is his distorted thinking that paves the way for his demise.

Be assured there is no conspiracy here. Just the powerful and the greedy and the scared acting in their best self interests. At the expense of the community at large. As it was in Bhopal. As it should not happen again. But that is up to you. Us. We who make these daily choices. Us with our astigmatic attitudes. Let us correct our anomalous astigmatism. Let us think more clearly. Let us choose the course more carefully. But now let us gaze upon Regin and Moana. In the child's bedroom Frea is fast asleep. Our little delicate Frea. Beautiful as a blossom blooming.

As delicate as a flower. She sleeps soundly. She sleeps peacefully. As only those with clear conscience can sleep. This is true of all children. This is true of Fadi. He sleeps soundly unencumbered by astigmatic anomalous attitudes. He and Frea the promise of our futures. How muddied the waters can become. The cook comes by and clears the dishes. Moana is grateful. Regin offers a curt but respectful smile. Shall we take our wine and watch a bit of television asks Regin. Moana nods. They get up and head into the living room. They sit upon a soft couch. Their buttocks now kissing the buttocks of long dead quadrupeds. Of the bovine kind. Rump against rump. But for some cotton this might seem zoophiliac. Perhaps even bestial. If this makes you uncomfortable as it should. It is repulsive. But we think nothing of it. Not without it being pointed out. But are we that removed from nature we seek necrophilia with dead quadrupeds. You think I jest. I do not. Perhaps it is more accurate to call this zoosadism. Yes. That is perhaps more accurate. There are plants aplenty for all our needs. And sadisms and bestiality have no part in the divine experience. In the soul's journey. But this is how perverted we have become. How far removed. We cannot see the wood for the trees.

Regin turns on the television. They have access to satellite TV. They watch the news for some time. Nothing but sadness and badness. Polluting the mind. After a while Moana turns to him. She holds her wine glass in her hand. It is ready to be lifted to her lips. At any opportune moment to whet the whistle. To steal courage. What have you made of the Lebanese allegations that shortcuts were taken she asks. It is difficult to remove oneself from the rumor mills. Though these rumors are based upon fact. Our man prefers to play dumb. Though he is not dumb. He is taciturn. And he will be tacit in these crimes against the Lebanese. But this is his way. His cowardly ways. What rumors are these he asks. Note he does not repeat the word allegations.

That word has fact attached to it. At least the aroma of fact.
Moana smiles. You know what I mean my love she says. There is
growing concern that Anzu has taken shortcuts in safety features
and in materials while building this refinery she says. I wouldn't
pay any attention to the rumors he says. He is still trying to
watch television. But he cannot. He turns the volume down
respectfully. He looks at his wife. How do you know they are
rumors she asks. It was started by the previous foreman he says.
A man by the name of Faruq he says. I am assured by head office
and the Chief Engineer of this plant that this refinery was built to
code he says. Perhaps the code is not very good in this country
counters Moana. Regin smiles at his wife. This is not a conspiracy
he says. If anything the conspiracy was with Faruq he adds. How
so she asks. Well you know we had to let him go he says. Moana
nods. We had to let him go because he was a rebel rouser says
our man. He was just trying to incite dissatisfaction amongst our
employees says Regin. I see said Moana. Regin turns his body
towards her. He is trying to impress his point. Look he says
putting his hand on her thigh. What benefit would Anzu have in
taking shortcuts he asks. It's too risky he says answering his own
question. Anzu is a company firmly committed to the future and
to its shareholders he says. Short term profits are not the focus
of Anzu. Our man Regin is riddled with lies. Like a house filled
with termites. He just can't see them. To be fair. He believes what
he is saying. But what he is saying is incorrect. Anzu is very
interested in short term profits. As are most capitalist
companies. It is the rare one that can see the future and focus on
it. Besides. Anzu is insured well against catastrophic loss.
Though this Regin does not know. He will find out. It will leave a
bitter taste in his mouth. But this he will swallow well with the
oil of promotion and wealth. I hope you are right says Moana.
She pauses to sip at her wine. To mull her thoughts. I am worried
she says. About what he asks. About your safety she adds. I don't

know what I would do without you she says. She lowers her glass and lowers her eyes. She does not like to think of these things. Nothing will happen to me he says. He pats her on the thigh. Anzu is a good company he says. They want to keep good people around he adds. This is not quite correct. They want to keep morally indifferent people around. Of which Regin is one. Though to be sure he has some humanity. He will feel conflicted. Moana smiles at him. How can you be so sure she asks. Because they have told me as much he says. I feel one hundred percent confident that this plant will outlast us he says. He smiles at her. It is the smile of uneducated arrogance. But he does not know this. They do not know that she will leave before him. She will journey on before he does. We have seen this. This was Fadi's doing on the subway in New York. But tonight she is a little worried about her husband. Tonight she is concerned for his safety. Oh the things that worry us. The many mirages of the mind. Those worries that tug at us like ghostly sprites that have no form. We worry about imaginings that never materialize. And yet that which we should fear is hidden from view. But we never need fear anything if we live righteously. And I do not mean to proselytize. This is not religiosity that I preach. It is common sense. The golden rule. If we treat others as we would be treated. Then nothing would burden us. One simple rule. A simple sentence. The answer is in such few words. Seven words. Seven is a special number. It is seen all over the place. The Old and New Testaments are riddled with it. But this is all coincidence. The same can be said for most single digit numbers. Nevertheless. Let us review these seven words. Treat others as you would be treated. That is your guidepost. This is your enchiridion. Your vade mecum. It is all you need to know. It is the answer to life's question. Why are we here. The rest is filler. And it is the filler that we get stuck in. If there is one thing you take away from Regin's trials and tribulations it should be those seven words.

The golden rule. I would not have a tale of woe to tell if Regin had followed the golden rule. It is simple. Sometimes not easy. But easier than the alternatives. We've seen the alternatives. The short term gains that ruin Regin. Be not like him. This I implore you. If you can heed my warning. Follow the golden rule. Whichever religion you favor. You will find this maxim as a tenet. But I preach. And that is not my intent. Though I do so only to press upon you the severity of not following this basic tenet. Life is easy if you do. Harsher than it need be if you do not.

I'll end this now. You have all you need to lead a virtuous life. But more than that. A life that will be fulfilling. Moana is slowly feeling comforted by our man Regin's confidence. They enjoy the rest of the evening together. They watch some television. They drink more wine. And when it comes to eleven they retire to bed. They make love. Life is all around them good. Life will seem good around them for years to come. But this is the nature of butterfly wings. These interconnected strings take time to vibrate and sing of their melodies. It is fifteen years before these strings whine and sing of tragedies. But on this night. This one hundred and sixty-sixth night in Lebanon. This night is bright with passion and love. And in Regin's heart he feels that his life has just begun. And it has in a way. Each day our lives begin anew. That we may reinvent and not misconstrue the errors for true. Gentle reader you have been a patient companion along this troubling travail. We are nearing the end. Should I say we are nearing the beginning. This is the font from which Regin's troubles spring. All at his own hand. All because he did not heed the maxim. Indeed his trials do precede him. He acted with wrong intention. He shut the voice of reason put it in detention. He did not start forth with the golden rule. And this was his greatest error. This is also our greatest errors.

But we must visit the one hundred and sixty-seventh day. We must see how this unfolds. We must watch our man Regin. See how he vacillates. How he wrestles with his conscience. How he mutes his morals for a little gain. Personal gain that will come to revisit him with pain. The morning sky is swabbed in baby blue. The torn cotton clouds smeared across its face. Ashfaq is up early. His shift starts at six on this early morning. Our man Regin is in bed still as Ashfaq makes his way to the plant. Regin will be at the office at half past nine. This is coincidence. These are things he does not notice. And this is a gift. For he is running late. His driver is running late. That is to his benefit too. At half past nine in a very straight line the plant ignites and catastrophe ensues. Regin is able to see the fireball from his home. As he waits for his driver. Sitting in the living room reading the paper. He hears the noise. But we get ahead of ourselves. We need to follow Ashfaq. We need to see more closely how this unfolds. Ashfaq is at work at six. This is when the shift is changed. He meets with the graveyard shift's foreman. They exchange notes. Nothing untoward has happened. No. It will happen quickly without notice. This is how these things are done. For a long time the plant has groaned. Like a dying old man. The dying groans that can go on for hours. Enough already. Be quiet. Be dead. This is sometimes what we wish. This is not unkind. Though it is not helpful. Death makes himself comfortable when he comes by unannounced. His journey leaves him weary. So he shuffles. He paces. He looks around. He drags a pointy skeletal finger up and down our spine. He plays it like a xylophone. This is sometimes his way. Not today though. No. Today he is in a hurry. Today there are ninety-three souls to be scooped up quick. I jest of course. Not in what will happen but in how it will happen. Death is a metaphor. In metaphors we understand life. And death. That is all. Death has no form. Nor capacity. Nor malice. Death is only the next door. Just a turnstile. All I mean to say. Dear reader. Is that the plant has long been waiting to disintegrate. The pipes have for many days groaned. And moaned. Like an arthritic spinster climbing a flight of stairs. And today is the day it will all come to an end.

Ashfaq has been at work since six. He is in the bowels of the plant. There are many metal pipes to this gangly beast. Like a multi-tentacled octopus frozen in time. Ashfaq is wondering if the plant does not protest too much. Does it groan more than usual. He thinks it does. But his nagging mind he muffles. He goes about his daily chores. He is grateful for the job. It carries with it great responsibility. It will buy him a car soon. These are the things he thinks about. He does not worry himself with the moanings of inanimate pipe. He has voiced his concern. He might do it again at another time. It is nine thirty on this fateful morning. Ashfaq is about to breathe his last. But he has several left. If we only knew the remaining count. Of our shallow breath. Would we not live more vigorously. I should think so. At nine thirty the pipes shudder. This is when a spark ignites within one of the pipes. The shut off valve. A safety feature is too slow in responding. An astute employee notices the problem. He yells for Ashfaq. Ashfaq has him manually turn it off. But the manual override is rusted. These are the shortcuts. The effort is too great. He cannot pull the lever. He does not have the strength. Ashfaq rushes over to help. They both pull upon it. It slowly comes down. But it is too late. The ignition has started a chain reaction. In mere seconds the oil and gas ignites in a giant ball of heat and explosion. Ashfaq is dead before he realizes it. Perhaps that is a small mercy. In his cozy living room Regin hears the rumble. He hears the explosions. Like distant thunder. He gets up and opens the main door and steps out onto the porch. He can see the large gray cloud. A mushroom in the sky. In the distance. He knows where it comes from.

The next days are spent in meetings. Regin is not meeting with Lebanese officials. No. He is meeting with Anzu Inc. officials. They have sent people to meet with Lebanese officials. Moana and Frea are flown home. Regin is assured that Anzu is guilty of no wrongdoing. Yet his conscience nags at him. Even more so when Anzu is unrepentant. They blame it on Ashfaq. They say the proper protocols were not followed. I lie. They do not say this. No. Regin says it. For the Lebanese people want to hear it from the man who was in charge. That was Regin. Regin says it convincingly. Though he does not feel it. It leaves him queasy. When no compensation is offered to any of the victims. And the Lebanese government is complicit. They are bought with some bribes. At least enough. So that compensation is not required. Some money is spent on clean up. A half-assed job. Another eight hundred and thirty-seven die. In addition to the ninety-three at the scene. Over the next few months due to poisoning. Pollution and contamination. Regin did not know Ashfaq well. But he had heard no complaints. In the years to come he learns the truth. That Anzu Inc. had taken shortcuts. That it was not Ashfaq's fault. But by then. Carefree living and opulence have muddled his mind. He no longer feels the nagging of his conscience. And this is his error. This is also when it is well known that Regin is the man for Anzu Inc. Not like the burr that Christian Camael has become. No. Regin is malleable. He is easily paid for. Though he does not think of it like that. And Fadi. Our little boy Fadi becomes a man. He too learns the truth. His anger is chaotic. But there is a man who he comes to know as Uncle. He helps focus this anger. He uses the power of Allah. The perverted power of a group called Allah's Army. It is here our young Fadi comes to learn of violence and retribution. And of his real enemy. Of the corrupt west. And of bombs. But he is not an evil young man. He comes to leave Allah's Army. But the seeds have been planted. In fertile soil. And he is ready to blossom. We have seen the results of that. We have seen the carnage that can blossom from a hate filled heart. But Fadi was a gentle boy. This you must understand. Fadi was a sensitive boy. I have said this before. He did not have a mean bone in his body. His parents. Ashfaq and Layla. They were pious people. The Allah they loved was all compassionate. All merciful. This is the Allah that Fadi knows too. But his hatred is bigger than compassion. His anger harder than mercy. And we know what comes of this. Not that we must excuse his actions. No. That is not what I mean. I only mean that by understanding we can come to different actions. We can take different paths. We can make different choices.

Codicil

Gentle reader. The story has been told. It has unfolded. We are at the beginning. At least at a starting point. We could go on. We could move even further back in time. We could end up at our man Regin's birth. We could venture further than that. We could visit his father's childhood. But what good would come of that. It would offer no further explanation. We are wont to blame things on others. Regin might have suggested. If you had asked. That his upbringing was too strict. That his father was a distant and unloving man. I jest. Regin would not suggest this. Though many of us might reach for these excuses. Like comfortable old shoes. Even if there is some truth to it. Even if his father was an SOB. Our man Regin made his own choices. As a man he made choices. And the fulcrum of his downfall. The gudgeon or hinge from which his life swung into chaos was wrought with his own hands. Our man knows this know. At the time he had an inkling. This is the conscience. The vigilant captain at the helm of our soul. Yet the boatswains are drunk below deck and the ship cannot be sailed alone. We end our story where our man Regin made his first of fatal errors. Understand. This was not one error. It was a myriad of them. A swarm if you will. One mistake does not a life ruin. But picking at scabs will surely leave a scar.

Compounding errors will lead to trouble. We have seen this. Dear reader you have journeyed with me. You can see it too. As our man Regin stood at that lectern. As he took no responsibility. As he blamed Ashfaq. Though not in as many words. As he stood as the patsy for Anzu Inc. This is when the butterfly beat its wings. Our man Regin mistook it for a gentle breeze. And fifteen years later. It was fifteen years later we saw him hanged at his own hands. That is where we have started.

We have come full circle. You can travel the world in a straight line. So it is said. And in a house in Paris that was covered with vines. Lived twelve little girls in two straight lines. These choices that our man made. The blurred lines. They can and they will intertwine. And it was this crossing. The line that wasn't drawn in the sand. The one he crossed over that led to the fall. It was not the apple that Eve ate that sealed their fate. It was the serpent. That voice that led her astray. That muffled the conscience that would have kept her straight. This too was the fate of our man Regin. Too many times he turned a deaf ear. Too many times he forgot the golden rule. But we who are left living. We can learn this easy lesson. Our man paid a dear price. Our price is nil. For this knowledge is free. This we know intuitively. I pray gentle reader that from his tale. From this journey yours may be error-free. And though one error does not a life ruin. It is a slippery slope that leads to lost hope. Even though there might have been confounding factors. Perhaps our man Regin was too eager for riches. Perhaps his poor upbringing caused embarrassment. Perhaps it was a spurned lover who fell into the arms of a richer man. These are all sidetracks. The fact of the matter was Regin made culpable choices. By his own freewill he took the thorny path to that high cliff. And with his last breath he leapt right off of it. How much easier it might have been. How much more straightforward it should have been. He knows this now. Our man Regin. May you not have these troubles. May you see the vibrations of butterfly wings. May they only ever sing upon harmonious strings. Take a page from this book. Take note to steer clear.

Yours

Regin Sigurd

About Jason Blacker

Jason Blacker was born and raised in the heat of the African sun. South Africa to be precise, a country complex, beautiful and scarred. He calls Canada his home now where he lives with his son and wife and four cats none of whom are called Pirate.

Although the winters are harsh the Canadian temperament is kind, hard working and empathetic. He writes both mystery fiction and literary fiction under the same name. As far as literary fiction goes, he gives a nod and a wink to the poets: Charles Bukowski, Dylan Thomas and Walt Whitman to name but just a few. Writers he admires and who have inspired him include Fitzgerald, Dostoyevsky, Tolstoy, JM Coetzee, Steinbeck and Hemingway amongst others.

His mystery fiction owes debt to the greats in the hard boiled genre of Hammett, Chandler and Spillane. He has a soft spot for the mystery genre in general and particularly enjoys Parker and Grafton.

Anthony Carrick was named in honor of his father and his heritage. Anthony and Carrick, County Donegal in Ireland, where legend has it, several hundred years ago the Blacker Kings of Ireland ruled benignly... a fun story whatever its basis in fact or fiction.

Jason Blacker enjoys writing poetry and he has a daily haiku blog where a newly minted haiku is offered up each day. You can find it at **HaiQueue.com**

When not writing he enjoys playing squash, running and painting and like the protagonist in his mystery novels, Jason spent a couple of years at the Alberta College of Art. He also likes candlelit dinners and long walks on the beach ;)

Jason loves to hear from his readers and fellow writers. You can contact him and keep up with his writing and publishing at his website **JasonBlacker.com**

www.ingramcontent.com/pod-product-compliance
Lightning Source LLC
Chambersburg PA
CBHW021425200626
46814CB00015B/1406